Duck!

Samuel Cornruff

Duck!

First paperback edition printed 2012 in the United Kingdom

A catalogue record for this book is available from the British Library.

ISBN 978-0-9575090-0-9

Illustrated cover and design by –

Chris Garrett, http://chris-garrett.deviantart.com

Published by Bongo Duck Publishing

For F and R

With thanks to CG for the cover, my reviewers
CG & AM, RL, FM

Prologue

How would you describe university students? The next generation of political high-fliers and the future magnates of commerce and industry? Or perhaps parasites on society, draining money from the hard working tax-payers and fouling city centres across the land with their wanton drunken and destructive behaviour?

The vast majority of people would side with the latter argument and choose to not spend any time thinking about them, opting to steer clear of that entire sub-group of society entirely. Some, however, find themselves unfortunate enough to be a parent or tutor to that most blighted of assemblages of young men and women but those that are not leave them to their own devices, in the process creating a hived off and utterly discrete sub-sector of society.

Occasionally unarranged meetings with members of this group are an unavoidable happenstance but anyone passing a gathering of the intimidating and normally vociferous students would not engage in conversation, merely giving a look of slight disdain whilst avoiding eye contact.

Young mothers with their babies in push-chairs would quicken their step in the local park, knuckles whitening as they gripped the back of the pram whilst urging their older, walking offspring to hurry along before the almost certainly inebriated youths set a bad example to their impressionable kin by smashing the wing mirrors of parked cars with hockey sticks or golf-clubs, the weapon of choice dependant on the exact nature of the pub crawl arranged by the student union that day.

White van-men would snarl or spit as they roared off in their filthy steeds with obscenities written (by those pesky students) into the thick dirt of their bodywork.

Pub landlords would grimace as the quieter Goth students hunkered in the dark corners of their 'local', counting out what remained of their free handouts from the government before sheepishly skulking to the bar to pay in coppers as the landlord grimly waited, taking out his aggression and disgust by polishing pint glasses within an inch of their fragile lives.

Coffee shop owners begrudged even the non-violent 'bookworm' posse as they slowly drank their cappuccinos with hazelnut syrup, sitting solitarily on four-seater tables tip-tapping away annoyingly on their laptops as they took more than full advantage of the free coffee refills and wi-fi access.

Secretly though, despite not understanding their ways and methods, most adults of a working age are bitterly envious of their youth and ability to be able to watch Countdown in the afternoon instead of slaving away in a boring office job, working for the 'common good'.

On the face of it, the three residents of 72 Haven Grove in the village of Steeple Hill were no different to any other of the aforementioned university students. To the untrained eye, each one of the adolescent tax-dodgers looked and acted just like the rest of their unwashed peers.

However, the young folk who lived in that particular humble abode were far from your typical students, not that they all knew that yet.

How they came to all live in the same house is perhaps a tale of fate, or maybe divine intervention by a force barely known and understood to an even lesser degree. On the other hand, was it simply a small matter of the rent? The let residence was renowned as the cheapest lodgings in the borough, for reasons known only to the mysterious landlord.

The house itself was at least common-place. A structure of stone and brick from the inter-war period, it resembled most of other abodes on the main road through the village, except for the sprinkling of much older houses that now appeared to be bullied and squashed into place by their newer and larger neighbours pressed cosily up against them.

Apart from a posh private school, an over-sized church (built with the help of a rich benefactor more than a century ago), a small pub and a hairdresser's boutique (that never seemed to open but somehow stayed in business), there was little else to say for the village itself.

Steeple Hill would have been pretty enough in its day but with the 'progress' of time it had become a suburb of the larger city of Bristol, its total submission into the urban sprawl only stopped by a motorway to the west and a deep wooded ravine to the east. At one time the church bells would have been the only loud sound heard by the local residents. Now their chimes had to compete with the main road being used as a rat-run for speeding commuters hoping to shave a minute off their journey times and helicopters buzzing overhead as they followed joy-riders in the nearby (and less salubrious) suburbs.

It was a very different scene five thousand years ago when the first settlement was established here, shortly after the last ice age when man returned to the thawing tundra. At that time the early Britons on the verge of the Bronze Age witnessed something bizarre and terrifying from their vantage point here on the hill.

That strange event was now ancient history...but they say history has a strange habit of repeating itself.

1

Stump used his muscular lips to lower the angle of the smoking pipe he held in his mouth so that the view of his dinner was no longer obstructed. With dismay, he examined his herring roll-mops on the plate below. He had feared the worst when the fireside chimney spewed a billowing cloud of soot unexpectedly in his direction. Alas, his concern was indeed founded as his favourite pickled fish snack was now coated in a fine layer of the black grains.

'Flippin' hec', Stump exclaimed as he woefully examined his persevered fruits of the sea for any morsels that remained unscathed.

Upon realising that his fodder was in fact completely sullied, any normal man would have eschewed the spoiled goods as to most they were now inedible - an unfortunate waste of food but one of life's little mishaps. Not Stump though. The belching chimney had so inflamed his frugal northern tendencies that he resigned himself to carefully removing the carbon that had deposited itself on his fishy prize by gently brushing the soot from the slithers of herring with his large hands.

Jack Steadfast Stump was a man living in the wrong place, at the wrong time and at the wrong stage in his life. This was epitomised by his rather unusual opinions on life that were unlike many of his peers (although this was almost certainly not entirely his fault and most likely a product of his most unusual upbringing.)

Despite being born in the Britain in the 1980's, the young Stump had been raised in Barnsley, Yorkshire, as if it had been a wholly different decade. This perverse upbringing was due to his father, also called Jack Steadfast Stump.

Jack senior was a grafter who worked hard for his living. A proud Yorkshire-man first and Northerner second who would ritually spit in the direction of soft southerners every day at 12pm. Described by most as a quiet and unassuming man, he married young to a nice wholesome local girl from the factory where he worked. She was not the prettiest of fillies but by no means plain. She was merely a good stoic lass, or at least that was what he thought.

As soon as they tied the knot, she of course quit her job at the factory to care for the family home. After all the man of the house was the breadwinner and the wife was the homemaker.

In married life, Jack was at first a content man. After work, he would come home and his dinner would be on the table and the house would be sparkling clean. After the evening meal, he would occupy the few hours until bedtime standing by the fireplace whilst fingering his braces and puffing on his pipe, the mellow, sweet smell mingling with the few bitter wisps of wood smoke that escaped from the hearth at his stockinged feet to create an odour that, to him, symbolized matrimonial bliss.

Then, something awful happened. Something changed. Or, to be more exact, it was people who changed. The year was 1975 and, five years late, the 1970's had finally arrived in Yorkshire. To Stump's horror and disgust the entire fabric of life as he knew it began to unravel. He first noticed it in his job at the factory where something called 'hi-tech' had entered the workplace. Honest, good–working Yorkshire-men were being laid off in their hundreds to be replaced by more efficient machines and strange contraptions with blinking lights called 'computers.'

With his place of work now a bizarre and foreign place, his home became his refuge where he sometimes relaxed by listening to music on the wireless set. However, in time, even the tunes they played on his trusty transistor became unrecognisable. The virtuous and soulful tunes of bands like the Beatles (before they became long-haired hippies) and the Everly Brothers were to be heard no more. In their place was a frightful cacophony of incomprehensible shouting youths with rings in their noses and brightly coloured hair.

Worse scenes were displayed on the streets of Barnsley - even the genders were becoming indistinguishable as men grew their hair as long as women and wore huge collars and patterned blouses.

Night after night Stump would return to the sanctity of his humble home (with the radio off), praying that it was all a horrible nightmare and that he would soon wake up, bathed in a cold sweat.

What had become of Yorkshire, his beloved Yorkshire, he thought with deep sorrow.

The final straw came when he arrived home one evening and opened the front door to be greeted by the most terrible of visions.

'Oh my Godfathers', he uttered as he stared in disbelief at his wife of so many years.

'What in the name of Saint Peter are you wearing?' He asked her, his eyes on stalks, not comprehending what they were seeing. His wife, his dutiful wife of plain looks and manner, was wearing a red dress, a bright scarlet red dress! Years of indoctrination about the 'Northern way' of puritanical clothing and this was how she repaid him? She knew full well the spectrum of worthy hues from which she was allowed to choose the livery of her wardrobe. She was allowed to wear white, any of the pastel shades, brown and of course black for church on Sunday, but she was never allowed to wear colours as brazen as this! Red was not the colour of a good wholesome bride, it was the colour of hussies or those 'ladies of the night' he had been told about in the big cities of Leeds or Sheffield.

This new stance from his wife was obviously unacceptable to Stump and he decided that something had to be done to restore her good old northern values. To that end from that day on, instead of returning home each evening, he would walk up to the barren wind-swept moors above the town, carrying large stones and rocks he garnered from the numerous disused walls that used to mark out the old field boundaries.

Every evening through rain, snow and foul winds (and everything else a Yorkshire summer could throw at him) he would trudge up to the high hills with his burden. The unfavourable precipitation would soak through his sturdy tweed trousers and cake his thinning hair to his brow but he pressed on, his pipe always clenched between his teeth, a man driven by his desire for a better and more pure life for himself and his spouse.

Several trips would be made each night until at last, after several months of hard graft, the collection of rough masonry at the summit of the moor resembled a pile that would make any quarryman nod in admiration. Then the real work began. Without any plans or blueprints and with no modern tools Jack Steadfast Stump fashioned a sizeable abode for him and his future offspring.

And so on one September morning, Jack arched his back proudly (not to mention painfully) and held onto his braces with a vice like-grip. He smiled broadly, (an expression that was almost imperceptible from his customary grimace) and admired his completed handy-work.

The abode was indeed a fine construction and he was rightly proud. It boasted six rooms on two stories with a chimney, a porch and even a small annex for the comfortable housing of ferrets. It was indeed an incredible feat as the only material used was good old Yorkshire stone and large quantities of elbow grease.

Jack Stump was a happy man again. He now had a home in which he and his wife could live far away from the evil temptations of the modern world with their bright colours and 'creature comforts' such as cotton, pre-made ready-to-roll pastry and, worst of all, television.

For a time relations between the gruff man and his wife appeared to improve. Indeed, not long after moving in Mrs Stump fell pregnant and in the bleak mid-winter a healthy son was born after a difficult labour. Difficult for Mr. Stump, the expectant father that is, as he had to wait around for ages and there seemed to be all sorts of unnecessary puffing and panting from his wife. 'How difficult can it be?' he thought to himself as his goodly wife tried to bring a new life into the world on the cold stone floor of their cold home with no painkillers or medical assistance of any kind.

In the end Mr. Stump missed the birth of his first born as he had had enough of his spouse's laborious shrieks and went off down the pub for a pint of mild, telling his other half to come down with his new son when it was all over. (The prospect of his child being a girl of course never entered his thinking).

After naturally celebrating his now obvious virility with other local friends at his favoured watering-hole, he decided to stumble home, reasoning he had actually been unfair to expect his goodly wife to join him so soon after childbirth. After all, he needed to remind his wife about the pile of ironing that was building up as that could hardly wait until morning.

He knew that as he staggered along the dark rural footpath towards his home that his wife would now have cleaned up any mess from the birth of their child and would probably be sitting by the fire tending to their new-born with one hand whilst perhaps chopping some vegetables for dinner with the other.

However, Stump's appetite and bonhomie was immediately quelled when he reached his front door. Pasted to the stone entrance (an ingenious design that hinged like a wooden door) was a note that had clearly been scrawled in great haste. At first the Yorkshire man could not coalesce the words in front of him into meaningful prose but once his brain allowed the shock to subside the message was more than enough to make any Northerner's blood boil.

The note read - 'I'm leaving you for a male hairdresser in London you twisted pig. The child is inside. You can bring up the little tyke how you like. It breaks my heart to leave him but every time I look at his little face, all I see is you staring back at me...Don't try to find me.'

On reading the bile-filled missive, Stump understandably felt loss and anger but it was a feeling of being an abject failure that rose up more acutely within him. Clearly he had not succeeded in returning his family to simple ways and a pure noble lifestyle. In fact his endeavours had resulted in the exact opposite as his wife's head had been turned by no less than a common effete coiffeur!

It had appeared that celebrating the birth of his son with his drinking buddies and not cooing over the new infant and mopping his wife's brow had been the final straw for his spouse.

Numb and unsure what to do for the first time in his life, Stump crossed the threshold and went inside. Blissfully unaware it was now minus one parent, the baby Stump gazed up in awe with his big brown eyes as a tear rolled down his father's craggy weather-beaten face. Just one tear you understand, because he was a man, but it was a tear nonetheless.

Over the next few days, depression gripped Stump senior despite knowing he knew he had to be strong for the bairn. In time his resolve gradually grew as he realised maybe all was not lost with the departure of his wife. In his son, barely out of the womb, he had the perfect pupil to teach the Yorkshire way from birth without distraction or evil outside influence. He would mould the infant in his image so that eventually he could be sent forth to teach the rest of England and the sinful Southerners the errors of their ways! And so he set about teaching his young prodigy from birth.

There are many lessons and stages required to turning a soft boy into a tough Yorkshire man but the most important that were dished out to the sprog were as follows –

Lesson 1: Tweed

A familiarity with tweed is vital as it is an integral part of the life of any frugal northerner. Its strength and durability means it can be woven into virtually any item of clothing and its thick hessian-like threads ensure it can withstand even the harshest of conditions on the moors.

It also had many other uses. For example, it could be fashioned into a hold-all that would take a surprising weight. Bed linen could also be formed from the material and, in times of hardship, boiling off-cuts in water for several hours over the stove would make a fibrous broth to warm the cockles during even the coldest of winters when vegetables were frozen solid into the ground.

(Naturally Stump senior also used the fabric for his baby son's nappies. Nappy rash was an initial problem from the sturdy substance but the infant's skin soon toughened to accept the rough material.)

Lesson 2: Tea

The drink known as 'tea' is practically a sacred liquid in Yorkshire. Served as dark as a coal-miner on a moon-less night covered in tar, it is the beverage of choice for people of the county, at least when the pubs and working men's clubs are closed.

Yorkshire even boasts their own brand of the once exotic brew, shunning the snooty Southerners who delicately sip the delights of

Darjeeling or Earl Grey. (It is a mystery why the folk of the county feel such a sense of ownership over this particular brand, especially when the plant in question is grown many thousands of miles away in India. But dear to their heart it is, of that there can be no question.)

To Yorkshire folk the action of making the tea is crucial to the finished taste. There is a clear method that must be followed, the teaching of which has been passed down from parents to their offspring through countless generations.

Firstly, the water must be soft. In Yorkshire this is not a problem as the water has been blessed by the almighty to ensure it will always be free of gritty lime scale that can spoil the sacred brew. Those Yorkshire-folk exiled from the fair county and forced to use water that is afflicted by the chalky residue must first filter the water or abstain. (Obviously abstinence is only a temporary solution, as a Yorkshire-man cannot survive more than a few hours without the molasses-hued fluid.)

Secondly, the brewing process. Tea should always be made in a teapot that is preferably of a traditional rounded shape with a subdued livery such as brick red or brown. The tea must be stewed for no less than five minutes to ensure enough effusion has occurred from the teabag to the surrounding water. However, the temperature of the liquid must never be allowed to drop below 200 degrees Fahrenheit. (To maintain this temperature, the pot can be temporarily housed within a tea cosy, as long as the design is not too floral).

Finally the brew can be poured into cups, as long as the required strength has been achieved. The 'spoon test' ensures the correct viscosity (and therefore potency) of the tipple. If a spoon can stand unaided at a 45 degree angle within the cup without resting on the sides then that be a fine brew.

Then all that remains is to pour enough cups for everyone (two mugs per person are required as one is never enough to quench one's thirst). The used tea-bags can then be retrieved from the pot and stored in a shallow dish for later use in at least two subsequent brewings.

Lesson 3: Cricket

In every other part of the country, the noble game of cricket is merely a sport. But in Yorkshire it is a way of life, nay a religion. Even before toddlers in that county can walk, a miniature cricket bat is placed in their podgy little hands to allow them early experience of wielding a mighty blade of willow.

Indeed whereas those soft southerners will provide their male offspring with blankets covered with ducks or small stuffed toys to carry round as comforters, Yorkshire boys find solace in a lump of wood with a leather grip.

Most lads are enlisted into their first local team at the age of four and the love of the game naturally grows from there as they receive an education that includes being taught about pull shots and googlies. (The females of the household of all ages are enlisted to provide the fare for the luncheon and tea intervals. The array of savoury and sweet goods laid out is expected to be extensive and varied.)

During adolescence (when the girls have advanced to perfecting the finer points of puff pastry and soufflés) the boys are being honed to play for the county side. Those that don't finally make the team are shunned by their fathers who will spend many an evening with their heads bowed by the fire-place, one hand on the mantle and the other solemnly packing a pipe, overwhelmed with utter disappointment.

Unfortunately for Stump Senior, his young progeny was one of those who failed to make the grade on the cricket field, but he was not too down hearted as he blamed the club itself for now allowing those born outside the county bounds to play for the famous 'white rose'. (Until 1992, those who played for Yorkshire had to have been born within the county but with so many 'outsiders' now playing in the team – how on earth did his son have a fair chance of representing his place of birth?) It was a decision that so angered the man that he ceremoniously burnt a bat given to him by the late great Fred Trueman himself as a protest. (It had obviously been his most prized possession.)

Despite his son's clear lack of cricketing prowess he now felt sure, as his boy turned eighteen years of age, that his training was complete. He would send young Stump junior forth as a missionary for 'Traditional Yorkshire' to educate the sinful southerners and show them the error of their ways by any means necessary; to teach the Yorkshire way and to make England re-born in the image of 'God's own county.'

Therefore, as a tender young sprat just on the cusp of adulthood, Stump Jr. was physically and metaphorically pushed outside the family home and out into the unknown. He cut a proud figure as he strode off into the mist on his epic journey, entrusted with recruiting more into the fold as he went and gradually transforming the country in accordance with his father's perverted willing. He was well equipped for the journey with a bag containing a large bottle of local (soft) water; several hundred tea bags; a dozen Yorkshire puddings and of course a range of tweed for all seasons.

First stop for the young man on the over-night train was London, the hub of all sin in our lands. However, unfortunately for Stump, the long walk to the local station at this late hour had tired him out and he fell asleep on a bench beside the railway tracks as he awaited his train. He awoke in a daze the next morning and in his haste and semi-conscious confusion he jumped on the first train that arrived at the platform, scattering his provisions of Yorkshire puddings on the platform as he scrambled onto the carriage.

The next thing he remembered was the train announcer heralding their arrival in Bristol. The West-country accent he heard over the tannoy sounded almost foreign to the ears of the Northern lad and he misheard the announcement as 'Brixton', a borough he knew to be in London from his father's teachings and he therefore disembarked to start his mission.

In a few hours he realized his error but it only took a quick walk through one of the more affluent areas of the city to determine that Bristol was in fact as good a place to start as London. Here Dandy fops were two a penny and many pedestrians he passed even appeared to be a little too 'light on their feet' for his liking.

After finding suitable accommodation, the young Stump decided to enrol at the local university to learn more about the evil ways of southerners before he began to convert the masses. But in time, without his father to guide him, he started to forget his vehement instructions until eventually only a strong chauvinist streak remained and instead of bemoaning maidens of their modern misdemeanours he filled his time with the linked pursuits of the quest for general knowledge and displaying his burgeoning intelligence at local pub quizzes.

2

Alex was not happy. Something was disturbing the carefully orchestrated order of his sanctuary or, in other words, something was wrong in his bedroom.

He was sat as he always did in his film director's chair, feet resting onto his soft leather foot stool and his right hand firmly gripping a half full wine glass (by the stem, never the bowl).

Normally he was relaxed in this arrangement of deliberately juxtaposed soft furnishings but at this very moment the strain he felt could clearly be seen, manifesting itself in the nails of his left hand as they dug into the polished pine arms of his chair. He glared at the cause of his discomfort, namely the glass cabinet in the south west corner of his boudoir. It was gently reverberating and therefore threatening to disturb its delicate and valuable contents of Bristol Blue glass. (He had painstakingly acquired the worthy collection of vesicles over the years and was not happy to see all that endeavour, not to mention money, endangered by some sort of vibration that threatened to smash his babies into worthless shards.)

Fleetingly he averted his gaze to the window, the frame handsomely bordered by fine embroidered silk curtains of a rich red hue. Their beauty was ignored as he looked straight past the hanging drapes and out to the roadside where his other prized possession was parked on the kerb. Ideally he would like his beautiful car to be safely housed in a garage but he preferred to spend that money on wine, his major vice and besides, the crime rate was reassuringly low in this part of the city. Still, it was with some relief when he saw that the silvery sheath protecting his pride and joy was undisturbed despite the tremors.

Some would say he treated his car like a baby and the analogy was not without foundation as Alex certainly had a special, almost fatherly, relationship with his car and it was one that he spent a lot of time nurturing. He kept the vehicle in pristine condition inside and out, washing the wings, waxing the wheels and giving the spark plugs a spring clean without fail every weekend. (It was almost a religious ritual. All his buckets and cleaning paraphernalia had to be laid out on the pavement by the car in neat lines before the process could begin. Passers by would smile wryly, smirk or snort but Alex cared not a jot as during these times he was at one with his car. (His cleaning materials even included babies nappies that he used to bring out a fine, smear-free finish that was so reflective he claimed young ladies would stop to check their make-up afterwards in the shimmering bodywork.)

But even the most scoffing of casual observers could not argue with the results of his intimate care. The finally tuned and well-cared for machine achieved speeds, acceleration and cornering that should have only been possible with a sports car many times its value and not from what many termed a 'hairdresser's car'. At times the connection he had with his self-entitled 'little sporty number' appeared almost telepathic, as if the car told him the exact moment to brake or turn the wheel.

Leaving the car references aside, Alex was also commonly described as 'an enigma wrapped in a conundrum clothed in GAP and Pringle'. This description would not be out of kilter with thousands of other students of his age who were from 'a certain privileged background'. The only difference was that Alex was most certainly not from that type of 'advantaged' upbringing.

As a young boy you could say he aspired to be something he was not, pretending to be from a super-affluent 'gated estate' rather than his reality of living in a 'hated estate'. More than that, in fact he believed he was born into the wrong 'family'.

Alex believed he was meant for higher things in life, right from the start. Although he was not born with a silver spoon in his mouth to smooth the sticky social jam in which the lower classes had to trudge through, he metaphorically stole one as soon as he could. He was not a juvenile kleptomaniac by any stretch of the imagination but he seemed to have an unerring, almost unnatural gift to be able to acquire the finer things in life, when such luxuries should have been well out of his reach.

Initially at primary school he was not academically superior to his peers and only achieved average marks. Despite this, scholarships to the best secondary schools were being talked about when he still had some of his milk teeth (the tooth fairy having paid well over the odds for the choppers he had so far lost).

He was not popular at school and this was probably due to his choice of attire. Other kids at his local comprehensive were loosely clothed in baggy ripped jeans and t-shirts whereas the young Alex glided into lessons donning waistcoats and occasionally a silk cravat.

In physical education lessons Alex did not aid his lack of popularity, scorning the more accepted pursuits of football and rugby for the love of more gentile sports such as hockey and cricket.

His lack of friends never seemed to bother the young gent as at lunchtimes he would happily be found sitting cross-legged on a bench eating ciabatta bread and Parma ham with ripe brie and olives instead of joining the other children in the dining hall messily wolfing down cheese and pickle sandwiches from home or burnt oven chips from the canteen. During playtime, his head would be buried in a good book, preferring the tales of Chaucer and other classic novels as the other kids in the playground read comics or played infantile games.

All these differences obviously singled him out from his adolescent contemporaries but for some reason he never suffered from bullying, somehow disarming his adversaries with clever verse rather than physical violence. Would be assailants would often walk away confused after a brief verbal battle instead of the fisticuffs they had expected. This was lucky as Alex was not built for warfare, being slight if not underweight and a tad short for his age.

At the age of eleven, the inevitable happened and Alex won a scholarship to one of the best private schools in the land. Here he at last felt at home. He continued to excel in his studies as well as cricket and hockey. He was even made captain of the school chess team. Oxford and Cambridge were naturally soon mooted as options for his next scholarly destination and beyond that, positions in the cabinet government would surely be his ultimate goal. There appeared to be no limit to what was possible for this gifted child, still only barely into his teens. However, some who tutored him had voiced misgivings, suggesting there was something 'not quite right' about 'that strange boy'. These views were occasionally echoed by others who met him, some experiencing an unworldly chill down the spine as they shook hands. A few even went as far as to raise suspicions against his impeccable character to a wider field but those that did oddly changed their opinion within a few days, seemingly without persuasion. (The couple of individuals that originally opted to pursue these thoughts further strangely changed their tune after impromptu personal meetings with the man himself.)

It appeared nothing would be able to stop Alex from becoming very successful and very rich. The world was becoming his muse and he was leading it a merry dance. Then one day something, or rather someone, threatened to unravel Alex at the seams as he fell in love.

A stranger looking at Alex would not expect him to be able to get any girl he wanted. Someone like him with average looks and an often abrasive personality does not commonly have the first pick of the most desired young ladies. Nevertheless, Alex had a 'certain something' that resulted him being able to boast a long list of conquests by the time he started sixth form. By that time he was almost tiring of the chase but one day a new girl enrolled, one that would distract him and beguile him almost to the point of madness and send his sky-high grades crashing through the highly polished floors.

He first noticed her one Monday morning, spotting her as she scurried between lecture halls, deftly weaving past the throngs of irregularly clustered students despite being heavily laden with dusty textbooks before disappearing out of sight. It seemed Alex was the only one who could see her and once he had, he wondered why nobody else had done the same. One fleeting glance of that pale face and striking clear blue eyes underneath her long dark locks was more than enough to ensure he would be forever transfixed by her beauty. He knew he had to have her and based on his previous experiences he assumed this would not be an issue.

With previous encounters originating from amorous intentions, Alex had never been backward in coming forward and would always make the first move without a flicker of hesitation but for some reason he found himself procrastinating where this new girl was concerned. Instead of going up to speak to her there and then he had let her go. Over the next few weeks he saw her from a distance countless times and followed her movements, going to her lectures instead of his, taking lunch at a table where he had a covert view of her and following her to the school gate when she finished her lectures for the day.

Eventually he overcame this foreign feeling of nerves and one afternoon he finally felt able to speak to her. He approached, she reluctantly looked up and he immediately stuttered over his opening words. Pausing, he regained his normal composure and found himself able to exchange a few awkward sentences that culminated in asking her out for a drink one evening, or at the weekend if she preferred. When the response was negative, Alex was surprised to say the least, his customary supreme confidence evaporated on the spot and he felt his heart shatter within him. Smiling beside his inner feelings, he bid the maiden farewell, determined to steel himself for another attempt at a rendezvous the next day.

Alex was distraught that he never got that second chance. The one girl that had so captivated him (and the only one that had spurned his advances) had left. Furthermore, nobody knew where she had gone. It felt stupid to think it as he barely knew her but Alex knew he had fallen for that mysterious girl.

At first, the rejection and sudden disappearance of the girl affected him badly. After all, it was the first person in his life that he had not been able to control. However, in time her memory became more and more distant as conquests in love, life and the quest for money and power forced the image of her deep into the recesses of his mind.

3

'I simply cannot believe you think they are the same Tarquin!' exclaimed Sebastian in his shrill but upper class voice. 'One has a cavity to be filled with meat whereas the other is mounds assembled on a flat base.' As if to metaphorically strike his point home, the tip of his pick struck the rock-face in front of him with some force as he attempted to gain a hold in the increasingly unstable cliff face.

'Yes, but surely they are of the same ilk, despite these subtle differences? Both are provided in equal quantities in all the parties that I have attended', retorted Sebastian, as he dug his crampon-clad right boot into a precipice to gain a good foothold enabling him to reach for a crag above him and hoist himself up another couple of feet.

'I am sorry, you are completely wrong. As an aside, I have to say personally I can't stand the ones that stink of fish,' murmured Tarquin as he returned his focus on his tricky ascent, his foppish blonde hair swaying as he hauled himself up another few feet and now finally within sight of the summit.

Sebastian was not able to reply as he had been distracted by what he could see in the rock in front of him. It was something that was uncomfortably close being only inches from his face. Confusion and then fear slowly registered across his expensively moisturised visage.

Above the duo on the top of the cliff a small duck could be seen quizzically peering over the edge at the well-to-do climbers below, cocking its head slightly to gain a better view. Any passers by would then have sworn they saw the diminutive bird shake its head slowly from side to side in an almost sorrowful manner as it looked down upon the novice mountaineers, but experts in animal behaviour would pour scorn on such an observation, stating that people often project human traits on animals and it was purely just such an anthropomorphism.

After a few seconds the bird waddled off in the direction of some nearby undergrowth, ignoring some stale bread proffered by a small fat child as the voices of the increasingly excited pair of climbers barrelled up the cliff face.

Moments later a tremor gently shook the ground. The quake was barely strong enough to be anything more than a curiosity to those walking in the park but it contained more than enough power to prise two young climbers from the adjacent cliff face and into the gorge below. Or maybe it had been the shock of what one of the affluent sportsmen had spied through a crack in the rocks that literally caused their downfall. Whatever the reason, the conclusion was that two brightly dressed fops fell to their doom in a tumble of expensive, garish climbing attire and flowing well-conditioned hair. Not to mention an unfinished argument concerning the similarities and differences between vol-au-vents and canapés.

Ironically, later that year, the Clifton United Nattering Troop (a clique of conservative ladies of a certain age) ruled at their annual general meeting that all canapés and vol-au-vents should be collectively referred to as 'amuse-bouches', thus making redundant the argument of the two unfortunate climbers who had by then long since passed away.

Some folk clearly did not warrant the nicknames they still had by the time they reached adulthood. Many were coined during an exuberant youth by their peers, relating to an event long since irrelevant to their more mature years. However, this could not be said of Terence 'Dusty' Green. He was a dishevelled looking man at the best of times, often resembling a plasterer whose slap-dash approach had resulted in the chalky slop residing more on his person than any walls and ceilings he may have been trying to smooth.

Despite this look, his powdery covering was not caused by any material of the trade but from mother earth itself. 'Dusty' was the grounds-man for the local cricket club and his appearance was simply because he spent so many hours in close contact with the turf and clod of the wicket and had little time (or indeed enthusiasm) for the futile process of cleaning his garments.

There was always something that needed doing to ensure this picturesque little village ground remained the pride of the parish and the envy of neighbouring clubs. Hedgerows that formed the boundary on two sides needed to be tended, the wickets had to be meticulously prepared with a heavy roller, the markings painted and the outfield mown at least weekly to maintain the bowling-green-like surface. Sadly though, at this present time any bowling ball was likely to disappear down one of the many holes that were appearing over Dusty's beloved turf. In fact the out-field was starting to take on the appearance of a billiard table rather than a cricket field – beautifully flat but filled with holes at regular intervals.

Tonight the diminutive form of the grounds-man wearily trudged around the wicket in the deepening gloom of the early evening. His footfalls sparked small clouds of dust to mushroom up from his sturdy (but hole-ridden) boots so that his dark brown eyes were the only discernable points of colour on his dust-covered form. Even from only a few yards away he must have cast a ghostly figure and that night he unwittingly scared many old dears who happened to look out of their windows from the adjacent retirement home. Despite their protestations of a ghost walking towards their home, their collective senility ensured that the response of their helpers in white coats was merely to administer another little blue pill to calm their nerves.

And so Dusty was able to continue unabated as he mused over his holey problem. He was pretty convinced moles were the cause of the small craters but if these particular scars had been left by the furry little critters, then these earthworks bore few of the characteristic hallmarks of their customary travails. For starters there were no mounds of freshly turned earth above each hole but just an opening in the ground leading away to a tunnel.

He had already tried everything he could think of to rid himself of the near-blind critters, even the old wives tale of using mothballs had little effect apart from the overpowering odour making the batsmen queasy at the crease on match days. Even ultrasonic devices, which were now all the rage, had dispersed the local youths (whose hearing still extended into the higher frequencies emitted by the devices) but appeared not to bother the furry worm-eating mammals.

That night, on closer inspection, Dusty realised the subterranean burrows were a good deal wider than the norm for a mole, or even the other most likely culprit, a badger. In fact, one could almost imagine a man being able to squeeze through these wider underground passageways but he could think of no reason why anyone would be inclined to do such a thing.

Regardless of how or what was responsible he vowed that at sunrise tomorrow he would return with the comfort and protection of larger weaponry and vanquish the unknown beastly foe that was messing with his prize-winning pitch. He decided that be it freakishly over-sized moles, badgers or something larger, there would be no escape and the field for the gentleman's sport will be reclaimed once and for all!

4

Hannah flung open her bedroom door with such tumultuous force that it cannoned off the adjacent wall and was almost freed from its hinges. She stood motionless in the now open doorway, smoke billowing around her imposing frame like dry ice around a singer at a pop concert. Her features were indistinguishable, silhouetted by the light shining through the bedroom window behind her. Only her smouldering flame red hair could be clearly discerned, the stiff ringlets snaking upwards as if struck by lightning. After a few moments of statuesque inaction she came to life with a jolt, flying across the upper landing and into the bathroom, plunging her head straight into the toilet bowl to quench her scorched head. A gurgled sigh could be heard as steam rose from the grimy bowl.

Hannah was the third and final resident at 72 Haven Grove but she was so elusive she made the yeti look like an attention-seeking socialite.

As far as the others were concerned, she he had begun living at the house at an unknown time, arriving from an unknown place and with an unknown agenda. In fact, the other housemates only knew for sure she was there at all because post in the name of 'Hannah Musgrove' would often arrive through the letter box. They would have dismissed the mailings as being for an ex-resident who had long since moved on if the letters and packages didn't mysteriously disappear from the doormat after a few hours.

Alex and Stump were even unsure how she managed to sustain herself as she never seemed to venture out for food or supplies. Her door was always firmly locked and she was never seen apart from fleeting glimpses of a night-shirt and its owner rushing to and from the bathroom after nightfall.

In addition, Hannah was never seen leaving the house or returning and certainly never spotted at the university where she was supposedly also a student. (In truth her poor turnout at lectures was a mere supposition on the part of the two boys as their attendance record was hardly superior). On this point however, the lads felt they always had good reasons for their shortage of hours in the lecture hall as the scheduling of lessons was verging on tortuous proportions! For example, the timing of early morning lectures (i.e. before 11am) was commonly grossly inconvenient as it was nearly always the 'morning after the night before' (aided and abetted by the criminally low prices of the 'Top quality' Bulgarian red wine sold by the corner shop down the road. Admittedly there was something not quite 'vintage' about the thin red liquid they quaffed, the labels having been adhered to the bottles with cheap glue and the taste bearing an uncanny resemblance to communion wine but budgets were tight and even Alex, the connoisseur of fine wines, had to hold his nose to save on pennies for petrol or new car shampoo.)

Of course afternoon lectures were also almost impossible to attend as, although hangovers had inevitably almost cleared by that point in the day, they clashed too much with a busy schedule of daytime television. (Woe betide the man or woman who denies Stump the opportunity to elucidate the 'Countdown Conundrum' in less than five seconds on the popular game show.)

At first Hannah was a figure of curiosity to the two boys who would wile away many a day attempting to encounter their elusive housemate. Subtle traps would be set and suspected viewings would be posted on the kitchen fridge with crude crayon drawings that attempted to capture her unknown likeness. But since she was barely ever seen in the flesh, these scribbled renderings varied wildly. Some depicted her as a larger than life character with long-flowing hair adorned in outlandish clothes and sporting strange futuristic jewellery. Other sketches supposed the unknown housemate as more of a cavewoman type, with rags for clothes and an unkempt appearance.

Of course in reality neither adolescent had truly known what she really looked like until this very moment. Stump and Alex cowered warily behind the banister at the bottom of the stairs. Hannah had been ensconced in the bathroom for some time but now she walked back out onto the upper landing and was beginning to slowly descend the stairs. Fear made the two lads want to run but curiosity urged them to climb the stairs to greet their secretive fellow tenant half-way.

The opposing urges cancelled each other out, their feet remaining rooted to the spot.

Their trepidation soon dissolved however as a pair of rabbit slippers came into view, the large ears flopping up and down with each ponderous but heavy step. They now knew they could relax - anyone wearing such childish indoor footwear would surely not pose much in the way of a threat.

Human legs followed the rabbit feet, the top of the thighs shrouded in a stained night-gown that appeared to be fashioned from a king-sized bed sheet. The female being came down another step and then two, an undefined expanse of waist and chest giving way to shoulders draped in tresses of flame-red hair. Her lengthy mane ran down her body before cascading down towards the dumb-struck young men who were caught in its spell like the Argonauts stricken by the sirens from ancient folklore.

Another tentative step and at last a ghostly pale face was revealed, highlighted by glassy blue eyes and a vacant comatose expression.

The (admittedly attractive) Gorgon like creature then opened her mouth but any thoughts that Stump and Alex had of the girl's first words being as memorable as the famous rendezvous between Livingstone and Stanley were soon dashed.

'Anyone got a light?' the bedraggled Medusa said wearily, producing a large hand-rolled cigarette of unknown composition from a concealed pocket in her night-gown. 'I'd die for a smoke.'

'You nearly did by the looks of you, woman!' replied Stump, finding comfort in these strange times by sipping from one of his two cups of scorching hot tea.

Alex decided to try to be more helpful and patted his pockets, producing a slim box of matches he used to light the fireplace each night. He offered the box gingerly to Hannah who extracted a single match, striking it expertly on the side of the box. Quickly she positioned the scruffy roll-up next to the small flame and inhaled through it, the cigarette swallowing the orange light greedily. Slowly she exhaled, blowing smoke rings past Alex who tried in vain to negate the resulting stench with a can of deodoriser. (He always had several placed in strategic positions around the house to facilitate the immediate expulsion of malodours such as this).

For the moment, Hannah appeared content to ignore her audience, her un-manicured fingers rapidly inspecting lengths of hair for damage from her fiery encounter but the examination was a cursory one and more out of obligation rather than any consideration for her appearance. Alex and Stump continued to crowd round Hannah at a safe distance, like schoolchildren on a trip to the zoo gawking at a rare primate whilst it groomed itself. The scorched young woman cared little for their captivated looks but eventually Alex decided her explosive entrance demanded an explanation.

'So....er, did we have trouble in the bathroom this morning?' he said, nerves causing his well-groomed eyebrows to inflect even more than normal when he asked a question but at least the silence had been broken.

Hannah blew another smoke ring, opting not to engage in eye contact before muttering her response. 'The bathroom was not the problem, it was the napalm. I think someone thought I was a mole', she said, almost amused.

Stump shifted uncomfortably at what he considered great insolence from this strange woman. The failure to respond to a man when questioned and her crazed actions that verged on the 'woman's mental blight' of hysteria would never have been tolerated back up north in his father's house. With his mug of tea he raised a toast to the great man turning north towards God's own county.

'Don't mind if I do!' said the suddenly rejuvenated Hannah taking the proffered cup of char in her spare hand, assuming the salute was in way of an offering.

Before Stump could begin to formulate a protest against the cruel removal of the tea in his possession, another tremor gently shook the house. Hannah looked up to the ceiling as if the cause could be seen in the boldly printed artex swirls, her relaxed expression evaporating from her face with the last of the steam from her head.

Remembering his manners despite the unusual entrance, Alex offered his hand as he made another attempt to converse. 'My name is Alex by the way,' he stammered, touching his chest with the flat of his left palm as if there was a language barrier between them. 'And this is your other housemate, Jack Stump.' This time he pointed towards the slightly rotund Yorkshire-man who could only manage a meek nod. Hannah accepted Alex's hand perfunctorily and automatically without shifting her gaze from the ceiling, still not feeling the need to engage in conversation.

Unabashed but beginning to wonder how rude this young woman was, Alex tried once again to eke out a response. 'Can you at least explain how you have managed to live here for over three years without being spotted?' As self-appointed spokesman for the house, he felt the need to seek answers and restore a modicum of order to this most confusing of days.

'What?' snorted Hannah, clearly more distracted than ever and trying to verbally swat the questions as if they were little flies buzzing around her head. 'Oh, that. There is a tunnel from my room to the outside world. There is a ladder down the chimney which I can enter from my room.'

'Well that certainly answers one query,' said Stump with a slight grimace as he brushed the last of the soot from his jacket, knowing how difficult it was to remove it from tweed.

A suggestion of guilt crossed Hannah's face as she looked at Stump's spoiled clothing. 'Ah yes, sorry about that. We really should employ the services of a chimney sweep but I find it's the only way I can be secretive and not to expose myself any more than is strictly necessary.

Changing tack, Hannah signalled an end to the line of questioning by clasping her hands together in a condescending manner. 'It's been lovely talking to you gentlemen but 'I'm afraid I don't have time for any more of these puerile queries, I really need to take you both with me so we can find the key and converse with the ducks if we are to have any chance of saving this city and perhaps the entire country!'

'What rot are you spouting now from your cakehole woman?!'
Stump said in angered disbelief.

Hannah paused before sighing deeply. 'Okay, maybe it is best if
I explain everything first but we will have to be quick'.

'Oh don't you worry my dear, I won't give you long to spew
forth your madness as I do not suffer fools gladly, especially those of
the female predilection,' Stump replied, waggling a finger under her
nose.

And so, Hannah prepared to begin her tale that would almost
defy belief.

If one was to say Hannah had been a shy child that would have
been a gross understatement. It was perhaps akin to saying that the
Himalayas are a 'bit hillier' than Norfolk or fish are not keen of being
out of water.

From an early age Hannah realised she felt different to everyone
else and became distant from all around her, even her parents. Her
mother and father did not really mind this reclusive behaviour though
as her development was otherwise well above average. She was
talking (to herself) and walking at such an early age that doctors and
paediatricians scratched their heads in disbelief and wonder. At every
step in her infant life the sheer pace of her mental development
continued to astound but her reclusive nature also grew with age and
her appetite for the written word became insatiable, Hannah much
preferring the company of books to people. She devoured papers and
tomes on all subjects but the resources on offer to her soon proved
to be woefully inadequate in quenching her unceasing craving for
knowledge. At primary school she found solace alone for a time in
the small library but became irritated when she had read the entire
collection in a matter of weeks and then had to endure the prospect
of having to interact with others who were so different from herself.
For example when her peers were swapping Garbage Pail kids
stickers, Hannah would be the only one collecting dinosaur stickers,
pretending to swap duplicates with imaginary companions.

Years went by and her brain continued to absorb information
like a sponge but little changed socially for Hannah. The young girl

became a teenager but even then she failed to succumb to any of the trappings that befell the majority of her fellow youths such as boys and playing truant.

Hannah continued to excel at the highest levels of academia, sailing through school and college before attaining a place at one of England's most prestigious universities. The only criticisms laid against her during her years of study related to her lack of communication skills and dislike for teamwork. However, as she continued to scale the highest echelons of scholarly achievement, most if not all of the few who met her dismissed her ways as merely a quirk of another genius. They thought that she was certainly not the first eccentric intellectual who shunned companionship and she would surely not be the last.

After easily attaining a 'double first' degree, Hannah started at the same university on a masters course but after enrolling on the first day she was seldom spotted during her supposed tenure of study. It was as if she scurried away like a rodent to find asylum amidst the huge halls and rooms of crumbling brickwork with its endless nooks and crannies. Rare sightings were made occasionally in the vicinity of the library but these were always unconfirmed glimpses. Her strange ways were accepted though as requested updates on the progress of her work sent to her email contact address were always responded to on time and the findings were enlightening is not occasionally 'ground-breaking'.

Her final thesis, as far as the university in question is concerned, remains un-submitted and unfinished whilst her whereabouts continued to be a mystery. Like the quest for Fermat's Last Theorem, the academic world waited impatiently for the results of her extraordinary early conclusions.

5

'Well, if we are all sitting comfortably then I'll begin', said Hannah, cracking her knuckles so loudly that it made Alex grimace. Stump did not feel the need to respond, preferring to suck at his freshly made tea noisily.

Hannah mentally prepared herself, swallowing one last pang of doubt about whether to share what she knew. Until now she had been reluctant to tell a soul about the threat they faced but, with time running out, she had little option but to trust them.

'Prepare to suspend your disbelief of the following tale gentlemen, for everything I am about to tell you is the truth. It may seem unlikely, fanciful and downright absurd but if you bear with me I hope to prove you wrong because I may need your help over the next few days.'

'But what can we do?' Alex protested, sweeping his hand towards Stump in a gesture of collective helplessness.

'You may well be surprised. I don't believe it is coincidence that we have all ended up in this house at the same time but I will elaborate on that later. First, I must obviously start at the very beginning.'

And so Hannah relayed a tale from 5,000 years ago when two giant brothers lived where the city of Bristol now stands, one named Goram and the other, Vincent. They were placid souls who lived simple lives toiling the land and residing together in a cave in the gorge below where the suburb of Clifton lies today.

All was well until one fateful day the quiet and contented lives of these siblings changed forever when a visitor happened to discover their abode.

As ever, both were working hard in a field that day, tending to the meagre plots of crops and vegetables that would help to sustain them through the harsh winter to come. Sweat poured off their brows as their pick axes came crashing down against the stony ground, the sound of the rhythmic strikes like the peel of two broken bells drifting across the barren landscape. In time though, they realised they were not alone.

Goram was the first to notice the new arrival and downed his tool to observe the figure that was nothing more than a dot on the horizon. But gradually the dot changed into a recognisable shape that slowly approached. Soon Vincent was also aware of the stranger in their midst and both brothers stood and stared, unsure whether to be wary or accepting. Was it friend or foe who was coming their way? (The brothers lived very solitary lives shunned or feared by the smaller humans. Seeing another of their kind was not a common sight in these parts.)

The figure edged ever closer to the brothers and as the moments passed they could make out more and more features of the outsider. The hair was most remarkable, being long, unkempt and as red as the heart of a roaring fire but at this distance there was still no telling who they were about to encounter. The foreigner was tall but clearly thin and possibly weak, maybe lost and walking for days in search of food in the fruitless expanses of the moor.

The frailty of the unknown traveller was soon confirmed as, when the gaunt form was barely one hundred yards distant, the creature stumbled to a halt, apparently unable or unwilling to tread another step. A shaking hand extended limply towards them, accompanied by a wide-eyed helplessness, before the red-haired being sank heavily to its knees. Finally, the last ounce of strength left the poor thing as its face met the ground with some force, the long red hair flying in an arc above the body before cascading down like the last flames of a dying hearth.

After a brief moment of pause, the brothers exchanged looks. Friend or foe, this was clearly someone who was ill, possibly dying and they desperately needed their help.

The brothers halted once more when they had traversed the distance to the stricken thing that now lay at their great feet. They could see immediately that whoever this person was, they may not live to see in the next day. Their feet were black with dirt and dried blood as they had no leathers to protect the soft soles from the hard and thorn-covered ground. The clothes they wore were barely more than tattered rags that were almost ready to fall off the meagre body. The haggard state of the creature was alarming but not the most surprising of sights as this notoriety was reserved for what they saw when they pulled back a tangled web of curly red hair to reveal the face of a woman!'

Now sensing this girl maintained her existence on this earthly plane by the very thinnest of threads, Goram took charge and instructed his younger brother Vincent to fetch some water, hoping to revive the stricken maiden.

Dutifully Vincent scampered off to a mountain stream that trickled over the incline a few yards to the west and filled a leather pouch he carried on his belt with the cascading fluid. He ran back and trembled with nerves as he held the pouch over the prone form of the girl. Goram snatched the pouch from him and slowly dribbled drops of water onto the face of the woman below. Her deathly pale and cracked lips gradually gained more colour with each gentle splash, the deep fissures becoming less prominent with each drop they absorbed.

It was some time before there were any signs of life from the helpless creature but then, just as they were giving up hope, they saw a slight quiver of the lips and a slow movement of her tongue followed by a gentle loll of her head. It was not much but at least she was alive and responding. When the pouch was empty Goram gently hoisted the young woman onto his broad shoulders. She was as lifeless as an animal carcass. The giant held her there securely as he began to walk back to the shelter of the cave, her long hair almost touching the ground as it swayed with each step. Vincent walked beside them, almost at heel like a faithful puppy following his master.

Many days passed with Goram continuing to care for the stricken young woman. Gradually there was some improvement but she remained unconscious for most of each day and night and brief moments of wakefulness were plagued by terrors and hallucinations brought on by the fever that gripped her despite the autumnal weather. Gorman could only look on as she tossed and turned, fighting imaginary foes with her eyes tightly shut, screaming words in an unknown tongue.

Vincent also dearly wished to care for the red-haired stranger but any attempt to do so was angrily rebuffed by his brother who clearly wanted to care for her himself. Resentment and envy slowly built within Vincent. Never before had he harboured such ill-feelings against his brother, who was his family, his mentor and his world. This mysterious woman had come between them.

Three weeks passed since the brothers first found the fateful maiden. She was now gaining in strength every day, sleeping less and eating more. She would sit up for hours at a time and sometimes even a smile would nervously appear on her face when Goram gave her a bowl of hot broth or prepared a new pelt to keep her warm. The smile would be reflected in Goram's huge face, a sign of the mutual warmth that had begun to grow between them, just as hatred grew within Vincent as he was increasingly being pushed to the periphery of this nurturing scene. He was becoming the outsider of the group, a cold lonely figure left alone to shudder at the edge of the cave when the other two shared the warmth of an intimate fire.

The weeks turned into months and autumn turned to winter in the cave. The three incumbents were often cooped up for days at a time in the small space, huddled away against the bitter snow-filled winds from the north. Goram and the girl kept each other warm as their bond continued to grow. Her trust in the great man blossomed but Vincent was still frozen out, like the fields he could see from the cave opening, with the last remaining hardy vegetables locked firm into the rock hard ground. Vegetables he and his brother had happily planted only that spring.

Eventually the girl felt comfortable enough to speak more often in her outlandish dialect. With much trial and error and fervent gesticulation Goram learnt a few of her words and they began to communicate but she would always refuse to talk about her past or how she had arrived on the moor in such a forlorn state. During the few times Goram dared to enquire about her past, the sparkle from her deep blue eyes disappeared and the smile was wiped from her face. The only knowledge she would share from her cloaked past was her name, Avona. Vincent was unable or unwilling to converse with the woman causing further alienation.

By the time the first green shoots of spring burst through the still thawing soil, Vincent had made a decision. He would win back Goram at whatever cost. He wanted it back the way it was, just him and his brother, the way he had always known it before that woman had arrived.

Vincent's plan was to take advantage of his brother's competitive nature. He would set him a challenge, one that would pit them against each other and rekindle the memories of their earlier (and for Vincent) happier days. It would be a competition that would consume each of them, forgetting all else, especially Avona.

Early one morning Vincent set off north with his pick axe without saying goodbye, (not that Goram and his love would have noticed his departure anyway), to begin the challenge alone. Oblivious to Vincent's purposeful departure, Goram and Avona continued their symbiotic and exclusive existence.

Some hours later, a distant and faint but oddly familiar sound reached its way to Goram's cavernous ears. It was a noise he remembered from, it now seemed to him, a very different time. He was suddenly alert to this new resonance, pricking his ears but otherwise remaining motionless, acting like a timid and vulnerable woodland animal, cautious but inquisitive. The faintest of smiles crept across his face as he was now able to recognise what he was hearing. He arose and started to run out of the cave, never looking back to Avona who gazed on with a bewildered look and outstretched arms, pleading with him not to leave her alone in the cold cave.

Meanwhile his brother Vincent laboured a few miles north, wielding his pick-axe with great strength and accuracy, endless great blows crashing down against the stony sod, creating a deep hole that he lengthened into a gully. Tirelessly he toiled, driven on by anger and determination and before long his channel snaked ever more southwards. After another few hours of hard graft the deep ravine was of considerable length and behind him dirty puddles formed where the water within the sodden ground had welled up. He stopped only once when he heard a deep rumble from the south. He downed his tool as the welcome sight of his brother Goram appeared from over a nearby knoll. Goram was out of breath but a beaming smile stretched across his moon-like face. Vincent smiled back. His brother was here. He had accepted the challenge! It was something they had talked about when they were children, both boasting that when they were fully grown they would be the victor. Now they would finally find out.

Goram turned and headed east to start his own ravine, attempting to dig deeper and quicker than Vincent and thus finish the challenge by reaching the sea before him. They both knew Goram was the stronger and always had been, so it was only fair that the weaker sibling Vincent had had the head start.

Vincent picked up his axe again with renewed vigour after seeing his sibling already making a strong start to his excavations. He struck the ground with a quickened pace knowing the race was now firmly on. His brother was already out of sight but from far away he thought he could sometimes here the faint sound of Goram's axe crashing down but only when the wind carried the sound in his direction.

Hours turned into days, neither brother resting for long in case the other gained ground in the race. At night each would use the stars and the moon to see by and to guide their way, only stopping occasionally for brief, fitful sleeps. Vincent soon became weary, pains shooting through his wrists and shoulders that contained swollen muscles converted into sinewy extensions of his body clamped onto the axe. He was barely conscious of the pain, driven on by sibling rivalry.

Finally one morning Vincent decided he could take no more. He knew his stronger brother would win but he was sure that these days of exhaustive effort would not be in vain. Avona would be forgotten by Goram and that was the real prize.

Vincent slumped himself against the bank of his ravine that was now a finger-like reservoir that had formed behind him on this lonely trek. He stared at the swirling water as it slowly collected around him, gradually creeping over his muddy footprints and pickaxe marks in the rocks. Mesmerised by the gentle trickling liquid he felt his eyelids growing heavy. He desperately needed a rest and decided to close his eyes for a few moments but just as he was about to drift off into a deep sleep, shattered from his days and nights of drudgery, he spied a white shape that fluttered across his field of vision. At first the weary worker thought a messenger from the gods had descended to take him from this mortal coil but his bleary half-closed eyes were deceiving him. It was merely a gull, a sea bird that had decided to investigate the over-turned earth in search of worms. At first the bird was nervous of the huge creature before it, cautiously padding through the mud and occasionally probing the earth for morsels but it soon lost its fear when it realised the exhausted Vincent was no threat. Presently more birds wheeled overhead, squawking excitedly at each other in the azure sky. Vincent drowsily squinted as he looked up at the winged beasts but suddenly his tired eyes widened as a realisation struck him like a thunderbolt.

He now forgot his aching limbs and blistered hands. The axe, which felt like a huge lead weight only moments before, was now as light as a feather as he struck the earth wall in front of him, sending the bird flying in a cloud of white feathers. After only three more mighty strikes the wall tumbled away in front of him and Vincent nearly fell over the mighty precipice that now stood at his feet.

The giant now knew that the seagull had been a sign. It had not been sent by the Gods but rather it signalled the coast must be near and therefore so was the end of his great challenge. With one final effort he had ploughed through the last of the soft clod, pushing the remaining soil over the newly formed cliff edge as the waters that built up behind him gratefully cascaded past to form a new waterfall.

Vincent looked down to where the water disappeared in a cloud of foam and vapour and then beyond to another sight he did not expect. It was not the sea below him at the end of the new river he had created but merely another valley but this gorge was many times wider and deeper than his own and at its base a familiar figure was striking his own axe against the brown mud, just shy of the sea itself. Of course it was his brother, obliviously working many yards below.

A broad grin cracked Vincent's mud-stained and sun-baked face. Without another thought he leapt over the precipice just as his brother made the final heaving blow that broke the flimsy barrier between his newly formed ravine and the sea. As sea-water gently flowed around Goram's ankles and continued to flood behind him, it was met by a gentle but increasing flow of fresh water at his back.

Goram threw his arms up as the two heads of water crashed together, mingling to form the estuary of the new river he had created.

Finally resting, Goram looked around and spied his brother on the cliff above him. Vincent ran across to greet him and they embraced in the frothing surf. Vincent had lost but this contest had never been about who would win. All that mattered was that Avona was now nowhere to be seen and he was together again with his brother.

Darkening clouds gathered on the hills above but the gloomy sky went unnoticed by the brothers until the first fork of lightning carved the sky wide open. Mere seconds passed before a second flash briefly illuminated the night sky revealing a figure on the cliff top above them, eerily lit from behind. It was Avona. Her features were barely recognisable from her dark silhouette but her fiery ringlets were unmistakable. Her arms thrust wide, she clearly beckoned Goram. Vincent's smile quickly changed to a grimace as his brother broke free of their platonic clinch and made off towards his love.

Vincent looked on angrily. Despite his best efforts, Goram was returning to this woman! He was enraged and picked up his brother's giant axe hurling it towards his brother as he raced away from him. The weapon cart wheeled through the air, stopping dead as it struck home, deep into Goram's back. He arched in shock and pain, falling to his knees before keeling over, dying quickly in the shallow waters without seeing his attacker.

Vincent, still full of fury, picked up the body of his brother and hurled it out into the river Severn where the body is said to lay to this day. Only his head and shoulders appear above the water, forming the two small islands of Steep Holm and Flat Holm in the Bristol Channel beyond the estuary of the River Avon.

Nobody knew what became of Vincent and Avona. Some say Vincent took his own life with the very same pick axe he used to fell his brother and that Avona can still be heard on a windy night in the hills about Bristol, weeping for her loss.

'Well that was a lovely fable Hannah…' said Alex in a wide eyed patronising voice, scarcely believing he had wasted so many minutes of his time listening to such tosh and flim flam. '…But just a couple of points if I may. One, I cannot believe any of this can be true, two, I don't see how this relates to the current unusual but perfectly explicable events and three, what on earth does it have to do with us?'

'These are all excellent points you raise Alex that I can explain in due course,' replied Hannah. 'But, sadly I do not have time to elaborate just now as we really must be going.'

'Give me one good reason why we should leave our humble abode and follow you anywhere this morning,' continued Alex, his hands sternly placed on his hips in what he hoped was an impudent fashion.

'Fine, I will give you three,' Hannah replied. 'For one, our rent was due last week and I know our last three cheques all bounced like rubber bands so I suspect the landlord could be here any minute rightly demanding the arrears. As rich as he is, I am sure even he would object to missing three months worth of rent. Secondly, the first stop we need to make is at the local pub and I'm buying. Thirdly, I have hidden Stump's entire stash of teabags and Alex, your favourite pink cashmere polo shirt. So, if you don't come with me, I will not reveal their whereabouts!'

After a moment of thought Alex responded. 'Well, the prospect of daytime drinking always disagrees with me but I always enjoy the argument!'

Unsurprisingly Stump concurred whole-heartedly as the notion of being apart from his tea for any length of time was unimaginable and the house was vacated in a flash, the students all leaving hastily in the direction of the local public house.

Hannah had guessed right about the landlord. He was on his way but, at that moment, overdue rent was not the most prominent thought on his mind.

6

It was early autumn in the city and a time of great change and reflection as the last warm days of summer are followed by ever cooler nights that start to draw in at an alarming rate. Jackets are dusted off from the closet and jumpers taken out of moth-ball filled draws. The gentile sound of the smack of leather on willow is gradually replaced by the guttural cries of rugby and football players whilst burnt holiday-makers return from far-flung sun-drenched oases, shivering as they disembark from their plane rides, unprepared for the sudden drop in temperature and the dour skies that clash with their garish Hawaiian shirts and patterned shorts. The rush hour traffic worsens as little Jonny (and thousands like him) return to school, driven the hundred yards to the gates in mum's eight-seater people carrier.

In Steeple Hill, the changing of the seasons was observed in a more subdued manner. Children threw sticks into the great horse chestnut trees to bring down the spiky baubles containing prized conkers and squirrels frantically hopped hither and thither, burying any nuts escaping the grubby mitts of the young boys. But squirrels were not the only ones to plunder nature's bounty as white-haired old grannies picked blackberries and damsons to make jams and jellies for the forthcoming harvest festival.

On the cricket field, Dusty Green put away his mower in the shed for the last time until next spring, laying the wicket to rest for the winter months, pleased he had at least scorched one of the strange creatures who had mined his precious wicket. The only shame was that he had failed to exterminate the vermin and the long-haired creature escaped by scurrying into its subterranean home.

In the rented houses of the village, students groaned as their alarm clocks awoke them at ungodly hours, the angry chimes falling on deaf ears as the contraptions failed to rouse their owners to attend their first university lectures after the summer break.

However, one student house was an exception that morning. Three alarms buzzed in empty rooms as an incongruous trio had already forsaken their warm beds and cold lecture halls to set out on a far more important (but largely unknown) endeavour. Stepping out into the unfamiliar light of day, the three housemates had unsteadily closed the door behind them and set out towards the local drinking establishment, The Masons Arms. Stump and Alex led the way to their regular haunt and Hannah followed on behind, looking furtively all around her, clearly uncomfortable in the open.

The Masons Arms was an unassuming place at best, a hostelry often overlooked by passing trade who sped past along the well-known short-cut through the village to reach the nearby motorways. Only a diligent few regulars frequented its interior that was concealed by small windows laced with blackened but intricate metalwork and smoky glass.

In fact there was little to distinguish the pub from any of the other stone-clad terraced buildings along the old street and only the sign above the door belied its function. Even this was largely covered by ivy that had spread from the sad hanging baskets that dangled precariously from their rusty fixings.

The old sign, which swung creakily on windy days, depicted a mason standing next to a river and shrouded in a loose, white worker's smock. He held a mallet in full swing, ready to strike a roughly hewn lump of stone at his feet. In the foreground a tree-lined river wended its way through a steep-sided valley. The whole scene was framed by what appeared to be a poem written on an unrolled scroll. Nearly all of the writing had long since become indecipherable, the letters worn away by the elements so that only the last few words could be made out. 'Released to the river, dead and gone', Hannah mouthed to herself thoughtfully as she approached the front door.

The pub may have been unappealing on the outside and the inside was sadly no different. This was no hidden gem overlooked by the bearded agents of the real ale guide books but it was at least an escape from home for the increasingly aged and grizzled clientele who were more than happy with the way it was, shunning other local drinkers who preferred the 'gastro-pub' at the other end of the village.

40

Although it was their 'local' it was only Stump who frequented the Mason's Arms regularly and even then only on Monday nights for their 'Quiz Night'.

To say Stump was a fan of pub quizzes was something of an understatement. In fact he had become rather an expert at it during his years in full time education. He had realised many years ago that his intellect, and an uncanny knack for storing useless nuggets of trivia, was the perfect combination for being able to succeed at these types of mental challenges.

What started as a hobby became quite a nice little earner for Stump who would even feather his nest of already handsome quiz winnings by making his valuable services available to other quiz teams. His reputation as a 'quiz hustler' soon blossomed until he had to be careful not to be spotted as a 'ringer'. To ensure he was not recognised, it would not be uncommon for Stump to wear a subtle disguise to alter his appearance or even to adopt a fake accent and he made sure never to return to the same pub quiz twice (apart from the Monday nights at the Mason's Arms where he always starred as himself).

Of course there were other factors that were needed to ensure victory other than Stump's intelligence alone, some more underhand than others. He had once considered writing down the secrets to his success in what would surely be a best-selling book but then he reasoned - why should he give the game away? However, a cunning adversary could gleam some of the more rudimentary guidelines from the tight-fisted tyke if he was buttered up in the right way with the purchase of a few pints of ale whilst his ego was lasciviously stroked. A pursuer of such knowledge would be furnished with Stump's three golden rules of pub quizzing -

1. Preparation - Know the quiz. Be the quiz. Find out what previous weeks have entailed. For example, the number of rounds and whether some rounds repeated each week. Ask yourself pertinent questions. Can a joker be used to double the points on one of the rounds? What are the strengths and weaknesses of your fellow team and their occupations and

hobbies? Plug the gaps in their knowledge by revising beforehand.

Underhand method - Does the quiz-master use a quiz book? Find out what it is and purchase the same copy. Analyse answers from previous weeks to ascertain any pattern to the questions used.

2. Know your enemy – Find out the team at each pub that wins more often than not. Try to pick a week when they are not there or under-strength due to absence. If they are in attendance, ensure your team sits next to them to apply psychological warfare during the questions. (See point 3)

(If you are not sure which team will win based on the scores from previous weeks, an educated guess can be made by looking at the teams present. There are a few generic types that always frequent such events –

'The third age'

Appearance - Grey of hair but still plenty of 'little grey cells'. Recently retired, usually all men. Probably technical experts in their fields, e.g. technicians, engineers, teachers. Wear bad holey jumpers in winter.
Drink - Rough cider or local ales.
Strength - A wealth of knowledge over a range of subjects and decades of personal experience.
Weakness - Popular culture, modern music and anything that happened after 1985.
Odds of winning - 2/1

'Tax dodgers'

Appearance - Garish t-shirts, worn in all weathers. A smattering of scarves and pashminas in the more 'well to do' neighbourhoods. Ripped jeans. The 'latest' fashion styles/accessories. Long hair. A bored girlfriend will quite often make up the numbers.
Drink – Imported lager from bottles, cider and blackcurrant or lime and soda if the monthly allowance from daddy hasn't arrived yet or already been spent on beer, value bread and super noodles.
Strength - At their mental peak, usually studying a variety of subject

matters giving a good spread of knowledge. (Even the 'token' females cannot be underestimated as days spent watching soap operas and reading glossy magazines will equip them with a good familiarity of 'celebrity culture'). Weakness - Not every university student is destined for more than a 'Desmond' (2:2). Music before 1990. Politics.
Odds of winning - 3/1

'The happy couple'

Appearance - 'Loved up' pair in their early 30's. No kids so free to 'pop to their local' in the evening for a pint or two. Sometimes join forces with another couple to make a four person team.
Drink - A pint of 'anything' for the man, vodka and soda for the lady.
Strength - Their love for each other.
Weakness - Hampered by a lack of numbers and shared experiences, their combined knowledge is often poor. (Gazing into each other's eyes, they lack the level of concentration required to be serious contenders and irk other teams when they ask for questions to be repeated as they were too busy 'petting' at the time).
Odds of winning - 6/1

There are other types of team but these can nearly always be ignored as front runners. For example -

'The workmates' may be regulars but this rarely gives them any edge - unless they sit at the bar. This may mean they are rather too friendly with the barman who allows them look at his answer sheet at every opportunity for a cut of the winnings.

'The family' may have a good spread of knowledge between them from different generations but the children may be too bored to contribute fully and if the parents were any good they would be in a better team with contemporaries of their own age.

3. Let the games begin! - Even before the first question is read out, the physiological warfare can commence. Pretend to talk to one of your team mates about previous victories in pub quizzes or, even better, national television shows but make sure you spout your boasts loudly enough so that you are clearly audible to the neighbouring tables. Whether your protestations are true

or false, this tactic may well intimidate some of the opposition. Try to make it believable though – Declare your former prowess on 'Fifteen to One hosted by William G. Stewart' or 'Countdown' rather than 'Mastermind' or 'University Challenge'.

The mental sparring can then take on a new twist once the questions begin.

Convince your opponents to make an error by excitedly calling out a wrong answer to a team-mate. You can even go as far as to write the wrong answer down in case anyone is copying your answer sheet, remembering of course to change it to the correct one just before the papers are swapped at each interval. (At this point you will see if the opposition are copying you as they will have the same correct answers as you but, most telling, the same incorrect ones.)

Another high-risk ploy could be to play your joker early. If you are confident of scoring approximately the same on each round, play your trump card as soon as you dare. It may demoralise your opponents due to your inflated lead and it may pressure them into hoisting aloft their joker early too, on a round that may not be their strongest.

If you are unsure about an answer, always go by your first instincts and the majority always rules. Never be swayed by a vociferous lone team-mate unless they are 100% sure with a water-tight argument. The many are smarter than the few.

Scrutinise the marking of your answers by other teams and question any contentious issues and 'half-marks' with the quiz master. You will rarely be marked down on review and quite often marked up.

Lastly, you will have to hope lady luck is on your side and, if you don't win, try to figure out why by going over the questions you got wrong so you can learn for next time.

Outside the pub the housemates paused with perhaps a little apprehension before daring to knock on the large and ancient oak door in front of them. Hannah strode forward the last couple of steps to the gnarled and cracked portal with more bravado than the fortitude she appeared to show. She knocked firmly, a short but distinctive pattern of taps, an obvious code for the recipient on the other side. Hannah stepped back and waited, carefully avoiding a hanging basket that hung no more as it sat sadly on the pavement, the forces of gravity and the recent small earth tremors finally proving too much for the oxidized bracket that once held it proudly aloft.

Seconds passed that seemed more like minutes as they stood exposed on the tatty doorstep feeling all too aware of what they were at that very moment – students bunking off lectures and trying to go to the pub before opening hours. Eventually a small hole appeared in the centre of the huge frame of the door, accompanied by a tiny squeaking sound as a peep-hole was slid open from within the dark interior.

'What do you ragamuffins want of me at this hour of the day?' said a deep, disembodied voice with a distinctive and thick Bristolian brogue, the booming nasal tone making the three housemates jump.

'We would like a pint of lager please' stammered a suddenly uncertain Hannah as she jutted forward pleadingly to the bare door.

Another pause followed but then, to the astonishment of the other two, this simple request seemed to pay dividends as the scraping sound of bolts being drawn and large keys being turned filled their ears. Alex was especially agog as although he possessed a renowned power of persuasion and an equally strong love of alcohol, even he had never been able to jar open the door of a public house before the allotted hour.

The large door swung open dramatically on its aged hinges to reveal the landlord who they hoped would permit them entry. Before them stood a giant of a man who was clearly perturbed by this unexpected visit. Despite being groggy and swaying slightly, he forced his sore and reddened eyes to squint as he closely examined his untimely guests, his pupils mere dark pin-pricks set well back under a protruding forehead edged with a thick black mono-brow. Above this his hair was equally dense and slicked back by a product that smelt uncannily like rancid butter.

As the unkempt bar keep jutted forward, the others instinctively leaned back, an action that unfortunately unbalanced the landlord and he came crashing down from the crate he had been standing on to add nearly a foot in height to his diminutive stature.

Once he had righted himself, dusted himself down and put his greasy follicles back in place, he ushered them into the bowels of the drinking hole with a grunt, revealing two lines of uneven and jagged yellow teeth.

'Apologies for the welcome', muttered the pint-sized publican as he disappeared behind the bar, 'One can never be too careful these days.'

'That is quite alright', Hannah replied in an even more clipped Oxbridge accent than normal, an unconscious response to the host's thick country dialect. Alex and Stump did their best to hide their sniggers at the barman's sudden loss of stature as the dirty oik reassumed his place behind the bar, replacing the battered crate on the floor to regain his artificial loftiness.

Remembering his manners, the barman slunk forward over the bar to offer Hannah his hand, presenting his side and bending down slightly in a submissive pose almost reminiscent of a fencing stance. A complex handshake between the two then followed (apparently of a Masonic origin) before a simple nod of the heads completed the greeting.

As Hannah reluctantly pressed flesh with the greasy barman, Stump busied himself by looking around the establishment. Even though he frequented this drinking hole regularly as a student in an 'old man's' pub he rarely spent time examining the interior. It was not the 'done thing' to look away from one's pint, or even the table top whilst you slowly drank your cloudy tipple in case you happened to engage in eye contact with a stranger. (Any such meeting of gazes in a hostelry like this was purely reserved for those sodden souls looking for a fight or gentlemen requesting a very particular type of liaison). But today, as the only patrons at this early hour, they could afford to take in the unique 'ambience' that today was even more special as the barman had not had time to tidy the tavern before their appearance. The result was a distinct resemblance to the Marie Celeste, if that ship had been run by Russian drunks.

A stench of sweat and stale smoke stubbornly filled the thick air so that the sunlight leaking through the moth-eaten curtains was barely able to pierce the gloom. Tables were strewn across the floor as if left in the wake of a tornado, some on their sides and others completely overturned. The carpet (of unknown hue or pattern now blackened from decades of muddy boots, spilled drinks and tobacco) was being further stained by the last dregs dripping from pints of abandoned ale, left in a horizontal position from the night before as if even the drinking glasses themselves had succumbed to the effects of the intoxicating liquor they had contained. Shadowy images from cheap portraits hung on the walls but they only looked on with disdain behind the soot-covered glass that protected them from all but the view.

In fact the only object left standing on the floor that did not need attention to correct its position or clean its surfaces was the fruit machine in the corner. It happily blinked away to itself, endlessly displaying its colourful and hypnotic cyclical patterns, oblivious to the disorder and chaos around it.

At least the bar was also fairly clean as if it was well above the tide-mark of the tsunami that had washed in the detritus below it. Here, on the top of the bar, the usual pumps were clamped firmly into place, catering for all tastes – namely five different types of scrumpy and two types of local ale of questionable brewing methods.

Lager drinkers often scoffed that real ales were made with dirt and twigs and men's beards but in this part of the world there may actually have been more than a grain of truth in that old wives' tale. Of course the 'true' locals who frequented the abode, often quietly asked for a more 'local' brew. At these times a furtive look left and right was always the well-practised precaution from the bar-keep before a pint glass would be filled surreptitiously below the bar from an unmarked plastic container. The liquid that arrived for the customer in many ways resembled red diesel - in taste, smell and the deteriorating effect it often had on ones innards. However, these dubious qualities never seemed to dissuade its loyal patrons, even if temporary blindness often followed a heavy session. The most popular batch of this foul liquid, a vintage from the infamously poor apple harvest of 1983, was later found to have had a dead rat floating in the barrel. On that occasion all agreed the deceased rodent had added some well-needed 'body' to the drink.

Behind the bar there was a simple but cluttered arrangement of accoutrements essential for a barman such as pint glasses and inscribed metal tankards owned the longest serving bar-props. These tankards were often etched with the name or nick-name of its owner and woe betide any other man who quaffed from them without permission. When the owner passed away, the tankard was retired, to be placed along-side its companions on the highest, dustiest shelf on the flaking wall next to the ceiling. Lying around somewhere were two chipped wine glasses and one solitary clouded brandy glass for the rare occasions when a lady or a man of gentry happened to wander in.

The barman hated cleaning glasses normally as he believed that a dirty glass was often of benefit to the taste of the cider held within it. (Actually, this was a lie, he was just lazy but this was always the excuse he offered on the odd happenstance of someone objecting to the grimy residue they found at the bottom of their drink.)

Despite an acknowledgement of his own laxidasical approach to cleanliness within his hostelry, this barman held an image of himself in his mind's eye that resembled one of those well dressed guys in the grainy black and white films from the 1930's and 40's where they would be cleaning a glass with a rag and a bit of spit as they nodded in agreement at tales of woe from its patrons, passing the odd sage comment. If our present-day barman had indeed try to adopt this character, it did not come across to his customers or was at least wasted on them. The required sage comments were seldom formed in his under-developed brain and besides, even his 'rough 'n' ready' clientele objected to him cleaning their pint glasses with his own spit.

Behind the bar, none of the modern trappings of today's public houses could be spied. There were no banknotes from exotic locations around the world and no boxes of crisps straight from the cash and carry with just the perforated circle ripped out of the middle. No packets of nuts hanging from the wall covering a scantily clad 'blonde beauty' in swimwear. In fact the only 'food' available for purchase was a jar of what was probably once pickled eggs and a bag of pork scratchings, the contents now long since fossilised in their thin transparent plastic coffin.

The barman concluded his mysterious handshake with Hannah and immediately looked more relaxed. 'My name is Levi, like the jeans', he beamed, unfortunately displaying his unhealthy choppers once again. 'Normally of course I would not be letting you in before openin' time but your lady 'ere exchanged the Mason's handshake and said the secret phrase about wanting lager so I am duly obliged to ya!' The last word was almost shouted as he rose another inch above the bar. Clearly this knowledge of the closeted underworld society and the resultant responsibility was a source of pride for the little man. 'Nobody drinks lager 'ere of course', he said with a sneer. 'We serve only the finest scrumpy and the odd pint of ale maybe, so it makes for the perfect code!' He smiled and bobbed up and down on his heels, obviously pleased with himself as he had followed his instructions to the letter.

Credentials reassured, the barman was able to return to his day-job. 'So, what can I get thee?' he asked, eyes wide, scanning the customers in front of him, instinctively reaching for the best of the chipped wine glasses as there was a lady present.

'A gin and tonic if you will my good man' tooted Alex unsurprisingly.

'And a pint o' mild for me-self' uttered Stump, for once forgoing his cup of char (but keeping the two half filled tea cups with him for later quaffing, no doubt rightly dubious of the water that would be used in the brewing process in this less than salubrious of establishments.)

Levi frowned and remounted his crate to reach a dusty old book on a high shelf behind the bar. A cloud of dust mushroomed up from the bar as he half placed, half dropped the heavy tome in front of him. It had been quite some while since he had made a gin and tonic (if ever) and he wanted to check the recipe before proceeding. If he was entirely honest to himself he wasn't sure he had any gin but he didn't want to disappoint his Masonic guests.

As Stump choked on the dust cloud, Alex vainly attempted to brush the settling particles off his expensive tailored linens. Only Hannah seemed unconcerned, using the distraction to lunge for the unused lager pump at the far end of the bar. By this point, Alex and Stump had long dispensed with looks of bewilderment at the day's events (for fear of their faces being permanently etched with a shocked look) so they let Hannah get on with whatever folly she was now engaged in. Levi, however, knew exactly what she was doing and as soon as he realised the young lady's intentions he flew himself towards the same handle, his greasy, lanky hair flying reluctantly away from his scalp as he ungainly dropped from his lofty position with his arms outstretched in a flagrant disregard for his own safety. His leap proved to be in vain as he fell on the wooden floor behind the bar, well short of grabbing the phallic lever of the pump. His eyes looked up just as Hannah used all her surprising strength to push back the bulbous and dusty metal knob.

The two protagonists stared at each other across the bar, chests both heaving from their exertions. Everything seemed as normal as before but both knew that something had been set in motion in the deep innards of the basement and it certainly wasn't the arrival of some lager from the beer tap.

Wrongly sensing all was well after this unusual interlude, Alex started to raise his arm to ask if there was the possibility of a wedge of lime (or failing that, lemon) for his gin and tonic. Levi vacantly turned to face the owner of the raised arm, the originator of the fruity request but before any words could be exchanged, everybody's attention was transferred to the fruit machine that until now had been quietly spiralling through its jolly programmed routine of flashing lights and tinny sounds and whistles.

The sounds emanating from the dilapidated machine were increasing in volume and frequency, second by second. It now played a rather captivating, rhythmic tune, accompanied by the circling lights that were shining brighter and blinked in time to the eerie, booming hum. The red, orange and yellow glow spiralled out from the centre of the large display and then back to a point, the pattern repeating itself faster and faster in a disorientating pulse of sound and light.

Prizes and jackpots were signalled but no coins were emitted from the gaping black mouth below.

The building began to shake as the noise and light from the one-armed bandit filled the room, dust entering the musty air as the heavy device liberated itself from its fixtures and fittings. On the shelves above the bar, glasses danced gaily, bouncing close to a perilous drop to the hard floor below.

The whole room was now vibrating violently and even the stone-work above the old blackened fire-place began to give way. At first gaps between the giant slabs of masonry appeared and then the bricks and stones themselves lost their collective cohesion, revealing the fireplace to actually be the bottom half of a small doorway. Beyond the new aperture, a pitch black corridor extended an unknown distance into the gloom.

Meanwhile everyone covered their ears and tightly screwed their eyes against the deafening sounds and flashing, blinding lights that flooded the space in the room like a bad wedding disco. But then, as soon as it had started, the overbearing stimuli ceased, leaving only a ringing in the ears and thick dust in the air that would take time to settle.

For once Levi was first to react, trying to splay his skinny frame across the new opening to bar any passage. He grabbed hold of two horseshoes that were nailed to the wall either side, his knuckles whitening with the strain as he affixed himself to the doorway. 'I am afraid I cannot let you past', he yelled, looking in Hannah's direction. 'You may be one of them Masons but it is more than my life is worth to let anyone enter this tunnel.'

This declaration was certainly not an issue for the other two males in the party who had no intention of entering a newly formed dark passage when there had been earthquakes that very day.

Unfortunately for everyone else in the room, Hannah had other ideas. Levi braced himself as she lunged towards the greasy man, trying to prize him away from the opening. She tugged at his scrawny arms, her teeth clenched and hair whipping back with the exertion but Levi showed equal determination, his arms and feet wedged firmly into the cracks and crevices at the edges of the walls almost like a starfish adhering to its moorings. The human echinoderm would not budge, despite Hannah easily being the stronger of the two and, finally admitting defeat, she spun round pointing in the direction of Alex, pleading for assistance.

'Alex, we need your help to get past. You need to persuade him!' urged Hannah.

Alex stayed put. He was never one to want to graze his knuckles and this occasion was certainly no exception. Besides, the fear of being hurt in any such resultant tangle with the publican was nothing compared to the more horrific thought of his expensive custard coloured designer polo shirt being caked in blood! A stain that would never come out properly, he despairingly mused.

'There is no way I am going anywhere near that tramp,' was the inevitable retort, accompanied with a slow shake of the head. 'Surely young Stump would be a much better choice to rough up this ragamuffin rather than little me?'

'Aye, not a problem' butted in Stump, who never needed much of an invitation to show off his prowess as a tough Yorkshire-man who did not suffer fools gladly. He slammed down his drinks of tea and beer and strode forward towards the focus of the argument, struggling to roll his sleeves up ready for the fight as he was wearing a particularly heavy tweed today.

'No, stop!' said Hannah, blocking his path with an outstretched arm. 'I fear our friend is not blocking our path by physical force alone, your strength would be no match for his powers.'

'Young lady, I think you'll find my skills which won me the Netherdale northern wrestling championships will be more than sufficient.' Walking backwards as he crowed, it was suddenly evident that Stump was making use of the full length of the room for a running leap at Levi the barman. He bounded through the public house and flew through the air in a pincer movement like a giant flying crab, ready to grab the squat creature in his way. What happened next was unexpected to all but Hannah. Stump confidently tackled the other man but instead of bundling the dirty publican into the even dirtier tunnel he merely bounced off the puny man, coming to rest in a dishevelled heap and banging his head on the edge of a table in the process, knocking him out cold.

Hannah sighed, her attention returning to Alex who was already backing away defensively. His intention was simply to run rather than employ a running leap of the sort just attempted by his housemate.

'I...I really don't think I'm the man for this job, I have to say' he vainly protested, one hand over his chest and shaking his head in a self-deprecating manner.

'Oh I disagree Alex and anyway, I am not asking you for your brawn, if that is what you are thinking.' The comment was proffered with almost a derisory snort that somehow made the young man relieved and emasculated at the same time.

'What we need you for...is your mind,' Hannah added, in what almost amounted to a hypnotic whisper. Alex stopped walking backwards but still looked on confused as Hannah pressed her point home.

'We need your powers of persuasion Alex. We need you to focus on moving Levi with your mind rather than your body.'

Alex laughed haughtily. 'I have never heard anything so...'

'Listen to me Alex and think about what I am saying.' Hannah interrupted. 'You do have this certain power and I am willing to bet you have used it many times in your life to get what you wanted even though you might not have realised it at the time. Think back to key moments in your life, was it just luck that everything has turned out well for you? The money, the education, success?'

'Not everything turned out well,' responded Alex absently, staring into the middle distance, thinking about one point, or rather person, in his life he hadn't been able to affect in his favour.

Hannah tried again. 'You must believe in yourself Alex. If you need any more proof, look down to your hand. What did you ask for only a few moments ago but thought you never got?'

'A gin and tonic' Alex said quietly, his mind not fully here in the present but replaying his life, looking back at past events with a new knowledge. Could that unkempt woman really be right? Had key moments in his life been determined by a mental gift of persuasion that others did not possess?

He broke himself from this spell and looked down to his left hand. To his astonishment, he saw he held a freshly made gin & tonic, poured into the only clean glass in the pub. A glass that only moments ago was empty and back on the shelf behind the bar. Alex briefly stared open mouthed at the clear liquid that effervesced gently with a wedge of lime flamboyantly impaled on the rim before knocking back the drink in one gulp to gird his loins. Yes, he thought. It was all starting to make sense.

Almost robotically, he pointed his free right arm towards Levi the barman who dismissively smiled at the posh student but within a moment that smirk had been replaced by a grimace. Alex squinted as Levi squirmed.

Nobody was near the barman at that point in time but somehow his firm grip was coming away from the opening as he lost his hitherto limpet-like purchase on the stonework. Gently he swung away, pivoting on his right leg like a well-oiled door. He could not turn his body, somehow stiffened like a long dead corpse, but he was at least able to swivel his head to see his departing customers as they made haste behind him and into the dark hole, the unconscious form of Stump being carried with some difficulty by the others. Levi only regained the use of his limbs again when the sound of their footsteps had dimmed and a sudden rock fall blocked the entrance behind them.

Alex stared at Hannah as their eyes all began to adjust to the gloom she had led them into. At the same time a spark of realisation crossed his mind as he pondered where the future course his life could now lead, if he could learn to use his power at will.

7

Stump suddenly found himself back home, back to the place of his youth. In the distance he could see the basic stone house built by his father's own bare hands using traditional methods. By the house he saw his old man, gaunt and frail with age but with an inner strength that shone out from his beady eyes. He beckoned his son with his Popeye like arms, a rare smile lighting up his face. Stump returned the smile, galloping ungainly towards his father, reaching out to embrace him well before he traversed the distance between them.

But he never finished crossing the gap between them as he was snatched from this happy vision by a comforting smell that lifted him from his dream. He awoke to find Hannah waving two his cups of tea under his nose, rescued for him before they entered the tunnel. Even though the contents were now stone cold, to Stump they were more reviving that smelling salts were to a concussed sportsman after a clash of heads.

With their return route back to the pub clearly blocked by large chunks of masonry, their only option was to press onwards, an idea that did not seem to faze Hannah at least. 'Now where were we?' she asked, possibly rhetorically as she brushed the hair out of her eyes so she could see what she was doing in the very dim light of the dank tunnel.

'Throwing some light on the subject might not go amiss' offered Stump, talking to a rocky projection in the wall he had mistaken for the female member of the group. Alex was deep in thought and offered no opinion of his own, seemingly unaware of what was transpiring.

'An excellent idea Stump,' Hannah replied absently as the corridor exploded into light from a tiny torch she carried on her keying. The light it produced was feeble but definitely preferable to the complete darkness that had preceded it. Despite the weak power of the torch it did provide a much improved impression of their new surroundings, even if it did make them want to tackle the large pile of rubble behind them and retreat back to the safety of the pub, rather than continue into the unknown of the tunnel.

Their way ahead now illuminated, they could see that the tunnel in which they stood was a perfect cylinder, no wider than two metres in diameter. It was of a worn brick construction, clearly designed to withstand great pressure from without and probably also from within. To all intents it appeared to be a stretch of old Victorian sewer, thankfully long since abandoned and made redundant although its scale hinted it was originally built to serve a much grander and older property on the site of where the pub now stands.

Alex and Stump were not sure why they continued to follow Hannah but follow they did, taking tentative steps into the tunnel that was now sloping steeply downwards. To pass the time, Hannah concluded her story of the giants as they all slipped along the slimy, curved floor. 'As I was saying, Goram and Vincent died that windy night, many, many years ago, leaving Avona alone on the moors. The end of the story you may think, but alas no. As Goram was dying from his brother's own hand he vowed to exact his vengeance one day and find Avona again, no matter how long it took.'

The tunnel widened slightly at this point, putting the claustrophobic trio at ease a little. They were now almost able to stand upright instead of bending double, except for Alex of course, who had had no trouble walking normally, due to his lack of height.

'Scholars disagree on when this retaliation will take place...' continued Hannah, '...but clues were left in ancient texts shortly after the time which, in my view, only point to one conclusion.'

'And let me guess when that may be,' snorted Stump as he stopped, hands on hips, yet again in utter disbelief.

'Oh yes, very soon young Stump, very soon,' replied Hannah, spinning round to face the northerner with her torch held beneath her face, possibly for dramatic effect. Unperturbed by his cynicism, she pressed on with her convoluted fairytale. 'I was once a common student just like you Stump, until I found this story hidden away in a dusty and forgotten corner of the library during the course of my readings. For some reason I became captivated by it. I saw truths in the fable where others just saw another fictional legend from the time of dragons and trolls and the like. I believed it, I believed it all and if I am right then unfortunately, unless we can do something about it, the worst consequences may all be realised. But there was a key part of the tale missing. Pages had been ripped out long ago by an unseen hand – pages that explained how to vanquish the agents of the terrible torment that would be wrought again this year. There were few clues that remained as to where those pages were taken or what was scribed into the rough leaves of pulped paper but I did not stop searching until I finally picked up the thread.'

Hannah reached into her pocket and retrieved a scrunched-up and slightly torn piece of photo-copied paper with some handwriting on it, in the form of poem and verse.

'This is what I have spent a decade looking for, weirdly finally finding its hiding place beneath the wicket of the village cricket filed. I risked my life for this, nearly being flame grilled to death by that nervous green-keeper. The hidden messages in this very prose not only show what is about to happen but also I hope how we can stop a complete catastrophe.'

'Well if it is all so important to the well-being of us and others, I think I had better read it out to everyone!' said Stump, snatching the tatty piece of paper Hannah had been waving around before unfurling it and reading it out loud.

Here in times of yore, where Bristol now doth lay,
A brother fought brother on the deep red clay.
Now for the fair hand of a stricken maid,
Not dark hair but as red as the blood of the victim laid.

And there they sleep until one day,
Hark, they will awake, when on the ground the leaves lay.
Fight he will once more on this land,
All for the prize of the young maid's hand.

Led by anger they will not care to see,
Lesser men in their way without the key.
It must be found and wielded with body and mind,
Now to stop the brethren and save humankind.

The earth will shake and buildings will fall,
Once the giants start they will not stop at all.
Avengement is sought and for wrongs to be made right,
Virtuous Avona must then be found by the fall of night.

One youth will help with a greater mind,
Not alone but with one who is fierce but his heart kind.
Ready to fight he will come forth,
Intelligent, a dreamer from the deep north.

Victory against the giants can be won,
Even if one life is given,

Stump finished reading the verse, right down to the torn edge.

'Well, if you can find a hidden meaning in this poppy-cock then you are a better person that I', he said dismissively. 'Besides, it looks as though you are missing a line or two,' he muttered as he thrust the poem back to Hannah.

'I have to blame the groundskeeper for that, the end of it caught fire but luckily I managed to save the rest'.

58

After what seemed like an age of tedious and slow trudging through the cylindrical tunnel, the passageway finally opened up into a large almost spherical shaped room that was eerily lit. The chamber was of an impressive size, being roughly the dimensions of an average semi-detached house. Hannah put her torch away and the others blinked at the curving stone walls that were easy to see in some detail after their eyes adjusted to the brighter and unearthly green glow. What they saw provided another footnote on a page taken from a book of weirdness that described their day to this point.

The bottom half of the space in the cavernous chamber (that Stump thought resembled the inside of a teapot) was filled with water to an unknown depth. It was a ghostly blue colour lit from far beneath its surface. Some light passed through the water, projecting dancing shimmering and ghostly shapes on the ceiling.

A narrow walkway hugged the circular walls just above the waterline, providing a pathway around the water to an open doorway on the opposite wall. On the walls ornate carvings could be seen, although most were too small and intricate to pick out any detail in them from a distance. Those that could be seen depicted ducks of various breeds and innumerable shapes and sizes, all engaged in some type of activity. The pictures were reminiscent of battle scenes but the figures shown were most definitely waterfowl and ducks, not humans.

That was not the most unusual thing on view however. That prize was taken by the living creatures that could be seen in front, around and above them. Everywhere the three intrepid explorers looked they could see actual ducks. On the walkway that curved away from them, in the water and occasionally even in the air, flying around lazily before they attempted ungainly landings in the glowing pool below.

There was something different though about these ducks. They were clearly not the ordinary 'common or garden variety' that you would find toddlers feeding bread to at the local municipal park. For one thing, there was clearly an organised manner to their movements. They would waddle with purpose or swim in ordered groups, almost in military formation. Even their noises seemed somehow more intelligent. The constant chatter of quacking was less of a statement but more of an opinion. Some quacked quietly but others loudly, as is laughing at a joke that had just been told. In fact it appeared the ducks were communicating with some sort of language of quacks!

Only a few of the water birds appeared to be more like 'normal' ducks, preferring to sleep with one leg raised or casually preening themselves, redundant or stray feathers being plucked out painlessly before floating gently into the water. More still practised their diving, swimming short distances before disappearing under the clear blue water with a small plopping sound only to re-appear on the surface with a splash in a different part of the pool. The overall impression was in actual fact quite relaxed, akin to a spa for weary souls in need of a little rest and relaxation.

If some of the ducks appeared unusual this was nothing compared to what the housemates saw in the centre of the room. There, sitting on a floating island partially bordered by reeds, was the largest duck ever seen by man (or indeed woman). From head to toe it must have measured twenty feet or more, towering over the group to at least treble their own heights. The sight would have been even more impressive (or perhaps ominous) if the giant duck had not been slumbering so that its length and height was shortened as it huddled on the island, its head turned through 180 degrees and rested it on its own back.

8

Lance Murdoch carefully combed his hair using the windscreen in front of him a makeshift mirror. It was probably the fifth time he had tended to his coiffured locks that very morning but he felt at least one of his hairs was out of place and that just would not do. But in his enthusiasm to perfect his raven black tresses, a careless flick of his stainless steel comb resulted in a small blob of pomade splattering his otherwise impeccable powder blue Armani shirt. He cursed as he attempted to remove the stain with a blue silk handkerchief that was neatly tucked into his jacket, a perfect 'pocket square'.

Young Murdoch, despite being the tender age of 25, was not a man of the 21st century like most of his contemporaries and peers of a similar age. In fact he openly desired to be from another time and another decade – namely the 1980's.

His interest and respect for this long gone decade of exuberance and excess was, he had come to realise, due to it being the period in his life when he was truly happy. It was a time when he had felt safe in the bosom of his family before he was prized unfairly away from them by evil hands. Therefore by living as if it was still the 1980's, he endeavoured to permanently exist in his 'happy place'.

Murdoch had turned back the clock and cocooned himself in a world of synthesised music, chauvinism and political unrest between the world's super-powers. He had nurtured this craving and it rapidly strengthened until it absorbed every aspect of life. For example, today the modern businessman wears lightweight suits that 'breathe' and are comprised of man-made materials developed in space whereas Murdoch donned power suits made of heavy cotton stitched by young children in an Asian sweat-shop. He also shunned the latest technology such as mobile phones the size of business cards and wireless headsets. Murdoch sported a 'mobile' phone that would give a brick an inferiority complex, complete with an aerial that often poked at the eyes of passers-by.

His chosen lifestyle did not always make him happy though as it caused him no end of problems. Some of these issues were not serious but certainly tedious. For instance, his prehistoric attitude to women meant his cheeks were almost constantly red due to the slaps he received from girls in the local bars. What seemed to him to be a perfectly reasonable chat-up line was often perceived to be inappropriate in these modern times. At least his favoured Old Spice aftershave seemed to soothe his battered visage after these attacks.

Other irritations the young 'wannabie' yuppie faced were usually concerned with trying to find the items he required to maintain his outmoded lifestyle. For example, in order to purchase his suits, replete with shoulder-pads, he was forced to hunt high and low in the numerous local charity shops. He also had major difficulties updating his moth-eaten filofax as he could never locate a map of the Tokyo underground for love nor money. (He had never been to Tokyo and would probably never travel to the Japanese capital but that was hardly the point as far as he was concerned.) In his view, every filofax had to have one as surely one day you might need to know that to get from Nishi-Magome to Shinochanomizu you would need to change at Higashi-Nihombashi.

Murdoch was a proud man, especially of his surname, primarily as he had chosen it himself. He decided long ago he had no wish to keep the same name as his family after what they had done to him so he chose his new name from two of his childhood heroes.

The first inspiration was taken from the eccentric character from the 'A-team' television programme. As a child he loved the way the four intrepid Vietnam war veterans were locked in a shed every week but somehow managed to use their skills and ingenuity to make a tank in under an hour using just a couple of wheels, a sheet of metal and a blow-torch. To Lance this showed what someone could do to single-handedly vanquish their foes against seemingly insurmountable odds with only a little intelligence and know-how at their disposal.

The second role model for his name (and indeed his way of life) was the famous antipodean media magnate Rupert Murdoch whose brash and unrelenting quest to add to his burgeoning corporation grabbed his attention as a youth.

Despite this rather challenging lifestyle, Murdoch now felt that he was not only comforted by his alter ego but that it also empowered him. And power was something he desperately needed to fuel his vendetta. He sought revenge on one family member in particular for his part in the injustices from so many years ago. He had patiently waited for the right opportunity and the means to achieve this deadly goal and now, purely by luck (or as he liked to think – destiny) he had found a way.

Murdoch angrily punched the windowsill in front of him with a clenched fist as he recalled the unfairness enacted on him and the dire consequences it had had on his life. It had taken nearly two decades to fight his way back up from the gutter and he would soon be on the top of the pile once again, usurping the one individual who had once struck him that near fateful blow.

'Stop day-dreaming Headroom and break down that damn wall!' screamed the tinny voice over the inter-com system into the cab of the heavy machinery where Murdoch sat. ('Headroom' was one of the kinder monikers given to Murdoch, after the virtual 1980's TV star Max Headroom who was famed for his loud power-suits, slicked-back hair, blinding white teeth and over-sized shades.)

Murdoch shrugged with visible disdain for his employer but obeyed his superior by nimbly operating the joystick in front of him that directed the heavy machinery. Looking down through the large windows of his demolition crane, he neatly swung the heavy ball on the end of the chain that hung some fifty feet below his polished leather shoes. He hated this work but he would enjoy this moment. He knew his zenith was near as he swung the ball back and forth, the heavy weight making short work of the remains of the red brick house he was tasked with obliterating. Murdoch definitely saw bricks being strewn asunder with the impact, but in his head he imagined that same weight swinging effortlessly into the skull of his intended victim.

The foreman stood a long-way below Murdoch, calling out instructions to him on which bit of the wall to knock down next but his worker was blatantly ignoring him now, focused on something quite different. Murdoch brushed his over-sized shoulder pads and slicked back his hair for the last time before determinedly pushing a lever forward, forcing the caterpillar tracks that the huge crane rested on into motion. The crane edged forward, its driver seemingly oblivious to the foreman who waved frantically before saving his own skin by jumping out of the way. With Murdoch sat at the helm, the crane bounced towards the hole it had created in the wall and scraped through the newly formed aperture and out onto the main road, swerving to the right as the huge wrecking ball swung in a menacing manner.

Murdoch's perfectly whitened teeth clenched as he leant forward over the simple controls of the wrecking machine as it careered down the narrow streets, somehow avoiding the bewildered pedestrians and drivers who were in its way. In his mind nothing was going to stop him now, not even a lack of pomade. Thus he resolved to even allow his hair to become even slightly unkempt if it meant achieving his ultimate goal.

Murdoch had had many years to plan his revenge. Anger and bitterness had risen inside him for nearly two decades, taking over his life and fuelling his 80's persona. Now he had bided his time long enough. It had taken many years to find his enemy again, a long and lonely search, but recently he had found where his foe has ensconced himself and now they would pay dearly for making his childhood a misery and creating the fabricated husk of man he had become.

Less than a mile from Murdoch's rapid but haphazard traverse across Bristol's streets, the cause of the earthquakes that day suddenly and terrifyingly became apparent to the commuters of one of the main roads into the city. Drivers on this particular route were already of a nervous disposition as they were spooked by the earthquakes that day in an area not known for such a phenomenon. They knew that the normally picturesque thoroughfare now took on a more ominous feel as the fragile cliffs loomed above them on one side and the river Avon below them on the other. Despite the new danger of falling boulders or the road breaking up and the fear of plunging to a watery demise, they chose to carry on with their normal routines, driving for work or pleasure as, after all, it was at least thirty seconds quicker going this way than any other route. The new threat to life made everyone drive faster than they normally would, rushing to the relative safety of the flatter ground outside the valley to the east or the west. The occupants fretted apart from young children who travelled without worry, sleeping soundly in their car seats, squabbling with siblings or being mesmerised by their favourite film played on the small screens embedded in the upholstery in front of them.

The collective anxiousness and apprehension exhibited by the adults was soon proved not to be misplaced, although for an entirely different reason. Atop the cliff where boulders had fallen in the earlier tremors, (sadly killing two dandy fops as they climbed the escarpment), something extraordinary began to occur as, incredibly, a figure started to emerge from the rock-face. Vehicles swerved on the road below to avoid those who had already stopped to gaze in awe. Children were excited at the view, too young to be scared or brought up on a life of computer games and CGI films, unaware of the real and not imaginary danger that faced them.

The jam of pirouetting cars and lorries soon became locked in place on the road in a cacophony of horns, late arrivals slamming into the back of those who were already there, exacerbating the twisting metal carnage. Now trapped, everyone desperately leapt out of their metal steeds, just as a giant fist burst through the crumbling stonework. Luckily there was nobody left in the jumble of vehicles as they were showered with stones and rocks of all sizes, falling like deadly, dusty hail.

Without a pause, a foot appeared at the base of the cliff, kicking a few already embattled cars, the force launching them unceremoniously into the shallow muddy waters of the river. The other adjacent foot duly emerged out of the rock but then there was no further movement, an eerie silence drifting over the unusual scene. The brief period of calm did not last long. It was shattered like fragile glass as the giant figure finally freed itself entirely from its rocky prison, its muscular arms and chest thrusting the heavy bedrock horizontally into the air as if it was mere polystyrene as its bulbous head rose through the top of the cliff, quickly shedding its temporary wig of turf.

There Vincent stood once again, feeling the cool revitalizing breeze on his face for the first time in a thousand years. Everything around him had changed in this time but this did not unsettle him as the shape of the land was the same. To him time had stood still and he had only one notion on his mind – to find his brother Goram and ensure that meddling Avona did not interfere with their happy and simply life again.

He looked due west to where he knew the body of his brother lay out in the channel between England and Wales. Vincent saw his kin was yet to stir in the waters but it would not be long before he would also rise. Turning his eyes away from the west he stepped up onto The Durdham Downs, a leap of a couple of hundred feet but just a quick jump to a true giant of his size. Once at the top he cleared his lungs of the dust from all those centuries with an almighty roar before bounding off downhill towards the marshy land where he last saw Avona, an area now long since drained and the city of Bristol founded in its place. Behind him he left a bewildered mother and child in his wake. Both stood frozen, the child's recently purchased ice cream forgotten but still gripped tightly as it dripped down the infant's arm. His bottom lip curled, the precursor for a long, terrified cry.

9

Even below ground a few miles north, Vincent's scream permeated the deep cavern to where three potential heroes stood at the water's edge of an underground lake, bewitched by their latest unfathomable experience. The sound vibrated through the water, causing gentle ripples to radiate around the subterranean hollow but the ducks on the water were largely unperturbed, merely bobbing up and down in a sinuous wave like corks floating on a gentle sea.

If the normal-sized ducks were unmoved by the subtle pulses the same could not be said for the giant water-bird on the small island. At first its feathers appeared to bristle in unison and then its one visible eye began to open, its scaly eyelid peeling back to reveal a large brown glistening orb. The huge mallard then opened its beak as if to quack but instead the avian creature emitted a loud human-like yawn that echoed off the slimy walls of the cavern, startling the other birds and interrupting their various activities.

Only Hannah was unsurprised by this, as she immediately attempted to address the outsized water-bird. However she was stopped before she could form her first word.

'I can only assume you have come to seek my assistance?' said the duck in a perfectly eloquent but rather nasally and raspy timbre, amusingly not unlike a famous cartoon duck whose trademark was a very particular speech impediment.

'Yes, yes, we have your honour,' replied Hannah as she bowed nervously in reverence whilst simultaneously poking Alex in the side with her elbow to stop him from laughing. All Stump could do at this moment was to point in the general direction of the speaking bird with one of his tea-cups in a questioning manner.

The duck looked over at the trio with some disdain. 'Well at least one of you has respect for me and my position. It is a shame that the others in your party are not as polite,' retorted the haughty duck as he attempted to roll his eyes as best as a duck could.

'I do apologise,' Hannah protested. 'I can only highlight their naivety as they are sadly not as knowledgeable about the legend as you or I. However, I do believe they are the two other heroes mentioned in the prophecy.' Again Hannah bowed but not quite as low as before, sweeping an arm to her right, pointing out her two companions. Stump and Alex looked first at each other and then behind them, hoping in vain that Hannah was not referring to their good selves.

'Well at least you are here now. I was beginning to wonder if any humans were going to work out the riddles in time to vanquish the giants. If only we had not entrusted the secrets to that damned drunken fraternity all those hundreds of years ago.'

'You mean the Masons?' said Hannah

'Yes, the Masons. At one time they were a venerable guild of mathematicians and skilled craftsmen but they have long since been reduced to a drunken coven of self-indulgent, small-minded, egotistical and power-hungry nincompoops!' The last word was said with perhaps a little too much vitriol, the duck lifting its head for emphasis and promptly bumping it on the cavern roof as spittle jettisoned from its beak. The duck hid its discomfort as it carried on. 'So, what skills do these two have to help us in our quest? Please show me what they have so I can tell you if mankind are still doomed or saved from the brink of destruction,' it said, pointing his shaking feathered wing to and fro between Alex and Stump.

Stump, now seemingly less perplexed by the giant bird, took this as a cue to step forward. 'Well, I can make a mean cup of tea and I have a nifty slog sweep,' he said, unashamedly showing off his Yorkshire pride for tea and cricketing prowess.

'And I always seem to land on my feet, metaphorically speaking,' Alex added vaguely.

Hannah could only look on sheepishly. Not for the first time she questioned her years of research poring over dusty volumes in darkened rooms. Everything pointed towards her two housemates being the ones who would manifest the required powers but she still had grave doubts as the evidence the two boys had exhibited thus far was impressive but hardly an earth-shattering display of mental or physical strength.

'You always land on your feet you say?' said the duck. 'Well let's see if that is really true!' The duck closed its huge eyes once again – although this time it was not intending to sleep but began flapping its wings, slowly at first but then faster and faster until they were a blur in the dim light. The moving wings yielded a weak breeze that touched the faces of the humans, carrying a smell reminiscent of a rarely-cleaned aviary, namely the musty earthy smells of fermenting bird seed mixed with the sharper acidic smells of guano. The wind soon picked up, turning into a gale and swirling in eddies around the circular walls. The reluctant heroes crouched down and braced their legs in a hopeful attempt to keep their footing but it was clear they were going to be swept clear into the air at any moment unless something extraordinary happened. But of course on this day of all days, that is exactly what did happen.

Alex slowly raised his right hand in front of him, leaning forward to counteract the bluster of increasing force that whipped around them. 'Stop!' he quietly whispered, his palm facing the over-sized water bird on the isle many yards distant. And 'stop' is exactly what the bird did. The wings froze in mid-flap and the frenetic frenzy ceased just like someone had pressed the pause button whilst watching a wildlife documentary. The huge duck was not the only thing frozen in the room though. Everything else was now motionless. The water that had been whisked into small waves and eddies was captured in time, crests perfectly formed like stiff white meringues. Ducks lurched at precarious angles on top of the waves or even suspended as if from strings in mid-air. The scene was like a snapshot of a tempest from an oriental painting daubed centuries ago, or a calendar from a Chinese restaurant from the take-away last week. Only the three visitors were unaffected, a fact that took them a while to realise as they dropped their arms that had protected their faces from the fierce typhoon that no longer blew and released the tension from their legs as they found they could stand normally once more without having to brace themselves against the strong wind.

Alex started to walk robotically out in front of him, pushing away discarded feathers that hung in the air. The others instinctively followed, walking across the top of the wavelets like a biblical recreation. As they traversed the small distance between the two platforms, the giant duck suddenly began to stir, first the wide eyes rolling from front to side to meet their gaze before its huge wings relaxed to settle neatly against its body.

10

Joe Badcock looked down forlornly into his ramshackle old fishing boat at the pitiful catch. He reflected it had hardly been worth the effort (not to mention fuel) of coming out on this dark autumn day. Shoals of fish were few and far between at the best of times on the Severn but the odd tremors had hampered things further by scaring away the few denizens of the deep that did stray into the shallow waters. He decided on one more loop around the small island, dragging his net behind the boat as it chugged along before he would finally call it a day and head for home. At least he had enough for 'her indoors' to prepare a good fish supper as he put his feet up in front of the fire to warm his toes as they poked through his poorly darned socks. There would be precious little else to trade for a pint or two at his local though. Even the 'imaginative' chef would struggle to create a extortionately priced seafood pie from the few ugly looking scraps of sea-life that flapped sadly in his bucket.

Joe packed his pipe with tobacco from his pouch and smiled, remembering the way his grand-daughter likened him to Popeye as he puffed away to get the old thing going. He loved his pipe and its many uses and positives it afforded its owner. For example, a pipe-smoker immediately gained an air of veneration and respect (and often intelligence) without the social burden of aloofness. (After all, this was a working-class way to smoke tobacco.) But there was much more to a pipe than merely using it to smoke. Other uses included being a instrument to hail down a taxi cab or a friend and of course the small wooden implement came into its own when a stranger asked directions. A quick chew on the shaft would concentrate the mind and when the smoker had determined the answer he could use the same shaft to point the lost soul back onto the right path.

The loose tobacco crackled satisfyingly like kindle as he brought a lit match to its surface. Taking the first deep puff, he lazily scratched the salt and pepper beard that covered the sallow skin over what was once a chiselled chin. The old boat lumbered forward wearily, almost reflecting the state of its captain, wanting to head back to port for a well-earned rest.

But barely had they creaked a few hundred yards more before the most bizarre event began to occur. A single glistening silvery fish leapt clear of the water and slapped neatly into the boat behind the mackintosh covered man of the sea. He turned and laughed a throaty smoker's laugh, surprised but not alarmed by this single happenstance. Fish were known to jump away from underwater predators and evolution told them the safest place was out of the water, knowing they would return to the sea a few seconds later and hopefully behind the confused assailant. It was just this creature's misfortune it had happened to jettison itself in the way of the old trawler. Buoyed by the hilarity of this small slice of fortune, the sailor trudged on through the shallow waters with a renewed sense of contentment, not hearing the sound of the wet sea trout as it acted out its last futile writhings. But then another fish arced into the boat from the briny not-so-deep, followed by another and another. Soon the boat was a seething morass of fish of all types, ages and breeds. Joe was shocked at first but then arched his back as he kept his hands on the wheel, laughing haughtily. He was not going to question this good luck as many odder things, as they say, had happened at sea. He would just use this luck to his advantage, paying for a round for all the bar props at the Masons Arms tonight and fill his freezer to bursting with fresh fish after his other half had made the biggest fish pie that would fit their arga!

Smiling broadly now, the old sea dog coaxed his creaking boat towards home, the old tug straining slightly against the sheer weight of the fish that covered every inch of the deck and the strange waves that had come out of nowhere, cresting and breaking in front of the bow. Moments later Joe saw the reason for the fish aiming for salvation out of the water as a huge creature rose up from the island behind him and began to walk through the sea, heading in his direction. It missed the trawler by inches as its huge leaden feet came crashing down right by the old boat, spraying water and mud all around. Joe's pipe dropped from his open mouth in shock as he stared ahead towards Bristol, which he could just make out through the mist and spray, directly between the giant's gargantuan legs. His home, a roaring fire, fish pies and a nice pint all suddenly seemed very far away, especially considering the great bulk that now lay in his path

11

Back in the caverns, the giant duck sighed sagely, exhaling foul air from the nostrils high on its bill, clearly not at all put out at being frozen in time by the posh, well-dressed but short young man who now stood at the tip of one of its reptilian-like feet.

'Well you passed the first test at least, so you may be able to get want you want and control the wonderful world of wildfowl,' hissed the duck with more than a hint of smugness and self-satisfaction.

Alex outstretched his trembling hands in front of his eyes and turned them over and over, looking for a physical manifestation of his new power like a newly transformed were-wolf looking for hair on his palms. With a sparkle in his eye he raised his hand once more hoping to repeat the feat over the great duck.

'Oh, I'm afraid that won't work a second time,' said the giant duck. 'I let my guard down on purpose to see if you could prove the legend and luckily, to your credit you did just that.' The duck acknowledged Alex as an equal with a bob of its head. Alex was now left somewhat crestfallen that his new found powers could be outdone by an oversized duck.

The strange creature pressed on. 'So let us get down to business shall we? Firstly, I will introduce myself. I am commonly termed the Duck Lord, not to be confused with the Dark Lord, but unfortunately you may have to deal with something like his sort later on. But I digress. Let me start by telling you about our role in proceedings. For centuries humans have ignored ducks as stupid waddling creatures that have no great purpose in the great scheme of things. You have seen us a mere cog in the chain of nature, at best just another insignificant tier of the food chain and at worst an evolutionary cul-de-sac. You are confident in these opinions and yet you people could not be further from the truth. For we are the guardians of humans entrusted with your protection through the eons after the epic battle between the two giant brothers not far from here. We were empowered by a great wizard to use our intelligence and great numbers to combat their return in the distant future, a time that is now almost upon us. But in order to achieve our goal we had to stay inconspicuous and meld into the background of nature, noticed but unnoticed, liked but not loved, independent but staying close to humans to be near you when we were needed again to rise up against the twin forces that now present themselves.

'Since ancient times we have accepted your offerings of stale bread to ingratiate ourselves, swum and defecated in your fetid pools and drunk from the same filthy water. We allowed ourselves to be parodied on your living room walls in a flying formation and most shockingly even sacrificed ourselves to be served on your dinner plates with plums, oranges and other various accompaniments! Our final sacrifice was to give up our echo to be less conspicuous, biding our time until this moment, our joint day of reckoning.

'Despite all these hardships we found it important to keep our sense of humour. When you think we are quacking loudly with each other we are actually laughing and chortling in our groups, revelling in the power of our vital role as protectors of all mankind. You humans know well of our easy life, oblivious and ignorant of the significant burden passed down through our generations. It's a 'duck's life' or 'water off a duck's back' you always say. If only that really was the case. Only the French seem to know of our importance but even that knowledge has been lost deep in the history of the evolution of the related languages. Whereas the English say 'quack' to describe our speech the French word sounds more like 'co-ahn', spelt c-o-i-n. Their word came about partly because of the sound but equally because they knew our value, each one of us being as valuable as a golden coin.

'We have tried to hide but we have not always gone completely unnoticed. Dark forces tried to clip our wings centuries ago, using black magic to hypnotise us and like ancient lemmings we were forced to cliff-tops and over the edge. Many perished but those that were stronger battled against those demons or were able to survive the drop. The elite descendants of those brave few are amongst us here today, their only shackle being that they are hampered by the need to always be close to water, a condition that the evil ones placed upon us all to restrict our movements.'

The duck sighed, as if pausing for thought. 'In decades gone by, I would have relished the opportunity for this forthcoming battle but unfortunately I cannot easily move from this underground cavern as I have grown too large to squeeze through these narrow tunnels.' The bird hissed, possibly with a note of chagrin. 'But today at least I can loan you my finest warriors to aid you in your cause. They are a loyal band who will use their avian skills and knowledge to fulfil their ancient promise by protecting you, the chosen ones. This will allow you to stop the tyranny that the two giants are unwittingly about to release upon us all. For they will not stop until only one giant remains standing, not caring what or who gets in their way.'

'How on earth are a 'little duckies' going to help us though?!' snorted Stump, with a scoff and a scorn, even parenthesising the term 'little duckies' with the middle fingers of both hands.

At that moment, if the giant duck could have smiled in a sly manner he would have done. 'Please, allow me to demonstrate.' The duck turned away from the group and faced his much smaller avian disciples. 'Swim forward my winged warriors, my webbed wonders, my fearless feathered friends,' it instructed.

Obediently and without delay, three of the ducks began moving through the turgid waters, rudely bumping others out of their way. The chosen ducks swam towards each other, nearly converging in the middle of the water before swimming in single file and then leaving the pool, waddling up a shallow ramp made of small tree trunks and onto the platform.

'Let me introduce you,' the duck lord continued. 'First we have Duffy, well versed in martial arts of many kinds.' The duck to the furthest left presented itself, leaping acrobatically a full three feet into the air, swishing its wings around in a vigorous but purposeful manner before neatly landing back on the ground with legs askew.

'Secondly, I present Donal, a master in the ancient arts of conjuring and magic.' Promptly the next duck in line brought its wings together in front of him like a feathered kung-fu champ before parting them again with haste, producing a bellowing plume of flame that extinguished itself as suddenly as it had appeared.

'Thirdly, we have Peking, the undoubted brains of the operation.' The third duck bowed humbly before producing a Rubik's cube from under its feathers and proceeded to solve the famous puzzle within seconds, showing great speed and dexterity despite being hampered by the lack of opposable thumbs or even digits of any kind, its wings dextrously manipulating the puzzle. Peking showed the completed cube to the group arrogantly before secluding it again under its downy feathers.

'The others here, in my subterranean abode are my foot soldiers but rest assured they are the cream of the crop, the SAS of my feathered forces if you will.' On cue, the other selected ducks saluted in unison, enjoying their moment of adulation.

'This is amazing, incredible, unbelievable!' whispered Hannah in awe. 'I must record this for the annuls of history!' From a pocket she produced a camera and began to take photos, flashes briefly illuminating the figures and forms around her but the startled ducks began quacking loudly before their master suddenly brought a halt to the paparazzi style antics.

'I'm afraid I can't allow you to take photos,' said the masterful duck, returning to his calm but authoritative oration. 'We have not managed to fly under the radar for so long by allowing ourselves to be exposed in such ways.' One duck at the back of the hall quacked a laugh at the play on words but his nasal guffaw was curtailed by a stare from its leader.

Hannah reluctantly returned the camera to her pocket but not without scribbling a few covert notes (for an award-winning thesis she would surely write at a later date) as she turned her back. Stump, however, was less than impressed by the party tricks they had all just witnessed. 'You expect me to believe these little birds are going to help us fight two huge giants, a hundred times their size? I guess at least they have fearful names', scoffed Stump with his arms crossed over his barrel chest, 'Two that sound like cheap Irish versions of famous cartoon characters and one after a dish from a Chinese take-away!'

'They may sound like joke names to you but us ducks do not have many role models to emulate.' The great duck replied, with more than a touch of indignation. 'I cannot vouch for Peking though', he added more quietly. 'He chose his own name and, to be frank, he is a bit quackers.'

Alex remained suspiciously quiet throughout the proceedings. He was ignoring the others as he smiled mischievously, unnoticed as he secretly practiced his powers by commanding small stones to jump into the water purely with the force of his mind. This he managed with mixed levels of success, the odd duck flapping out of the way of the small projectiles when some stones skewed off at unexpected angles.

At the other end of the cavern, the great bird cleared its throat, ready for another proclamation. 'The time has come my warriors,' he said with gravitas, folding his wings over his chest. 'You must leave where I cannot follow and press on to the last stage of your quest to defeat the giants and protect mankind.' Turning back to the humans, he continued his tidings. 'The ducks will of course protect you, although I am afraid your journey may not be the most comfortable. For starters you cannot be seen above ground now with the giants already on the rampage. If they see you, they will surely try to kill you if they realise the threat you pose to them. All I can add as I bid you fair well is that you must try to choose the right path. Good bye and good luck to you all.'

The huge duck closed its eyes once more, a signal that it would utter no further verbal instructions. The trio of humans remained enveloped in confusion but the elite ducks plainly knew what was expected of them. In total it was twelve avian athletes that had emerged from the masses, Donal, Duffy and Peking joined by nine others that were 'different' from the rest. Wordlessly they split into three groups of four, each small cluster clamping themselves to one of the startled students. On each person, two ducks clung to each shoulder, holding on securely with their webbed feet and strong wings looking a bit like fat parrots on a pirate, the other two ducks attaching themselves to one leg apiece. Meanwhile all the other normal ducks had ominously left the water, clambering onto the concrete surrounds or flying to the ceiling to find a lofty perch.

Suddenly, beneath them the dirty water started to gurgle and spin, slowly at first but then faster and faster as if a giant plughole had been opened at the base of the pool. Without warning the twelve special ducks secured to the trio of humans took flight, their small bodies somehow lifting the two lads and lass elegantly off the ground (although not so elegantly in Stump's case whose extra muscular weight did hamper proceedings somewhat). They hovered over the whirlpool with their heavy loads before they all plunged into the centre of the swirling, foaming waters. The last part to be seen of the small gang was Hannah's long red hair, twisted into what looked like coils of rope on the surface before they too were sucked under the waters.

Just as the trio of teenagers thought they would surely drown, they were thrust to the surface once more, gratefully inhaling great lungfuls of the still fetid air. Their respite was short-lived however as they were now caught in the strong churning currents of an underground river, unsure of their surroundings and even more unsure of how to extricate themselves. At least, after the initial complete submersion, they were able to mostly keep their heads above water as they circled around each other helplessly, riding a watery carousel. Also caught up in the maelstrom were the twelve special ducks, none of whom remained attached to their human allies.

Each of the students tried to deal with this hazardous situation in their own way. Stump was doing all he could to keep his cups of tea above the frothing waves and Hannah tried to gather her long hair as it was threatening to strangle her. Alex desperately tried to steady himself as his lighter frame was being buffeted from wall to wall.

Down and along they flowed for what seemed like minutes until the waters calmed a touch as the ancient water-slide widened and the levels of light increased slightly from the twilight gloom. They all took the chance to catch their breath in the comparative calm and tried to gain their bearings in the lessening gloom. The waters were still too deep to gain a footing and too fierce to swim against so they span in gentle circles, clockwise and anti-clockwise as they bobbed, almost like plastic ducks in a river race.

Without warning their vista changed. Some distance ahead they could see the tunnel forked into three different, equally dark and uninviting openings.

'It appears we have a choice ahead of us!' shouted Alex, straining to be heard above the din of the thundering culvert.

'I wish I'd made the choice to stay indoors this morning instead of ending up here, that's for sure,' grumbled Stump.

Ever the thinker, it was left to Hannah to figure a way out of the situation. 'Well, it appears we are faced with not one choice but three here gentleman, as I am discounting trying to swim back up the tunnel against the currents.'

'I am going to pick one and swim towards it,' said Alex. 'I am sure they'll end up in the same place anyway.' He fought against the strong eddies in the stream, heading towards the middle of three dark circular apertures in the wall and disappeared with a strange sucking sound.

'Wait a minute!' said Stump, thrusting a finger out of the water to make a point which almost sent him toppling over backwards. 'Didn't the duck say we must choose the right path?' Without further ado, the strong Yorkshire lad powered his way towards that opening.

'Yes but did the duck mean right as in direction or right as in correct?' Before Hannah could make up her mind she lost her footing and tumbled head-first into the left of the three tunnels.

12

The centre of the ancient city of Bristol was now in chaos, a veritable no-go zone as innocent folk screamed and scattered, attempting to find refuge from the imminent danger that was now befalling them all. Indeed there was no escape from the spotty teenagers who hawked needy charities they'd never heard of and no hope of solitude from the vociferous men who proclaimed the word of God through cheap microphones. All of this was of course played out against a backing track of pan pipes and homemade R&B tracks played from huge aging ghetto-blasters. But even these terrifying irritants were ignored when the first eagle-eyed shoppers spotted a giant figure using the multi-story car-park as a step to gain higher ground in this low-lying part of Bristol. The fabric of the strong but hollow structure creaked and sagged as the giant figure of Vincent used his perch to look out over the rooftops searching for his Avona.

The first calls were labelled as 'mischievous hoaxes' when they were received by the emergency services control centre. Only when a dozen calls had been taken was the issue escalated to the relevant higher authority at Whitehall in London. Unfortunately that higher authority was out on a 'long lunch' with his counterpart from the Ukrainian civil defence unit, a rather attractive 26-year old lady called Ola. As the "grey suit" was absent, the responsibility was automatically delegated to a 18-year old intern on unpaid work experience who could find no reference to 'giants' in the government protocols. Unsure of what to do next (or whether he was being set up as the new boy) he decided it was best to wait until his boss returned, confident the issue could wait until then.

Just a few streets away from this chaotic scene, Lance Murdoch bounced along in his unusual mode of transport. He sped down one of the few remaining ancient cobbled streets in the city, a route he soon regretted due to the lack of suspension provided by the wrecking crane he was driving, the jolts and jars causing his hair to fall out of place and obstruct his vision. But in the end his product-laden follicles did not protect his eyes soon enough as, towering above him less than half a mile away, was the back (and indeed backside) of a huge giant! Obviously shocked at such a sight, Lance took evasive action to stay hidden from the beast, performing a sharp left turn down a narrow side street, causing the wrecking ball to swing dangerously back and forth in the process. On he thundered with the protection of the tall buildings to block his view of the giant (and more importantly the giant's view of him!) He careered past the lines of terraced houses that jutted into the sky, before he hit the main road, gaining speed along the straight tarmac that followed the river.

Lance swung his head from side to side as he motored, desperately trying see past the pendulous arc of the wrecking ball in front of him to catch a glimpse of the thoroughfare ahead every few seconds. He knew he needed to turn off the main road soon and onto a steep passageway that appeared as a gap in the cliff face to his right. He knew the junction was soon but he could not remember exactly where it was, being a road he did not travel along very often. The swinging ball continued to block his view every few seconds as he searched for the gap in the cliff, the pattern continuing for the next few hundred yards, the view constantly and hypnotically altering in front of his dark beady eyes – road, wrecking ball, road, wrecking ball, road, wrecking ball, giant, GIANT! It had taken a few swings for Lance to awaken from the trance of the wrecking ball swinging with metronomic consistency across his field of view but his survival instincts eventually overcame his stupor. This time he was not only fearful at seeing the giant again but he also berated his luck at choosing the same road as the giant to travel on. Misfortune seemed to follow his every move in life but until now he had not been unfortunate enough to have a giant blocking his path. Yet now, today of all days, here there was one threatening to play havoc with his carefully planned itinerary of revenge!

With his right hand on the wheel Murdoch used his left to slick back his hair as he considered his options. For some reason he thought that always looking immaculate helped his decision making processes, especially in a crisis. It always seemed to work for James Bond anyway! Suitably steeled, he quickly decided his only real recourse was again to take evasive action. Unfortunately, it was unclear at first what that action could be. Following the road ahead would only bring him on a collision course with the beast. He could now see the turning up the steep cliff between him and the giant but even if the hulk didn't pick him up like a toy car before he reached it there was every chance the beast would just follow him and squash him like an ant. He could turn back but the beast would surely outrun him so he needed to find a way to give himself more time and to stop the brute in its tracks for a while.

Murdoch looked back and turned his head left and right, scanning the scant cab for anything he could use to save his metaphorical bacon. Alas there was nothing to quell his despondence, just a rather large tub of pomade rolling around behind his seat. But then an idea struck him. Ordinarily the gelatinous substance contained within would not be of help in this situation but he knew this was no ordinary hair product! With a modicum of hope restored, he gripped the steering wheel with his knees to free his hands, using them to grab the tub and scoop out as much of the glutinous substance as he could. Arching his arms back, he held the gloop aloft like a pair of fully sprung catapults awaiting their release. Looking ahead he could see that the distance between man and beast was quickly being eaten up as their combined speed brought their inevitable meeting nearer. Murdoch held his nerve as long as he could but as the great shadow of the giant engulfed him he dared wait no longer. The umbra swelled around him, heralding a gigantic foot ready to crush his trivial form. Murdoch yanked at the wheel and lurched his heavy machinery to the right as his spring-loaded arm eschewed his gooey projectile in the path of the ugly beast.

The giant placed its heel obligingly on the discarded pomade and dramatically lost his previously firm footing. Even such a tiny amount of ultra 'wet-look' gentleman's pomade was enough for the huge shape to come crashing down to earth before rolling and slipping off the riverbank and into the waters below. The wake that followed fashioned a mini tsunami to ripple up the river, causing the large boats by the deserted waterside to bob up and down like corks in a bucket. Further up river the old SS Great Britain creaked in its dry dock as if yearning to get back onto the open water. There were no surfers though to take advantage of the first Avon boar, a phenomenon more accustomed to the larger river Severn.

Lance Murdoch made good his escape, knowing any time gained from the giant's tumble would be short-lived and the beast would be angered at its embarrassing upending. With the way now temporarily clear he pressed on, not daring to look back as he turned up the road that clung to the cliff side, his progress slow and laboured up the precipitous highway. In fact the machine he drove was really beginning to struggle up the steep incline, the gears whining alarmingly as it slowed to a snail's pace. Thinking the giant must be gaining ground, Murdoch finally plucked up the courage to look over the precipice to his left and immediately regretted his askew glance - for there below him the giant was already righting itself in the river and shaking a meaty fist firmly in the direction of the young driver. The gargantuan began to run – leaping from river to road in one bound and climbing up the steep green slope next to the winding road where Murdoch slowly crept, flattening trees between the two of them as if they were mere matchsticks.

Murdoch's response was to floor the pedal to the metal in the battered wrecking truck but his pilfered means of transport only gave him an ounce more juice and even then with begrudging reluctance. Despite the lack of power at his disposal, at long last he made it to the top of the hill, swerving violently to the right to take a thankfully flat road, a graceful avenue of tall trees. He gradually picked up some welcome speed as the ground levelled out, a timely boost as all too close behind him there was a distinctive metallic twang as the giant's fist made contact with an old road sign near to where he had been moments before. Murdoch ducked instinctively but for now the danger had passed as he gained some breathing space between himself and the giant. He knew the beast would easily catch him though when he broke into a run so he frantically looked around for some sort of refuge or hiding place.

At first he could see only chaos as it reigned in the affluent suburb he had entered. The local well-heeled and well-to-dos had hastily shortened their saunters and promenades, abandoning their pashminas as willing casualties they could well afford to lose when they had caught sight of the giant. Aging playboys passing in their sports cars careered into the distance, thankful of their eight-cylinders and Wankel rotary engines that enabled them to leave the scene with haste, even if their toupees flew away, revealing their balding heads shining from out the top of their open convertibles and leaving their much younger female companions to wonder if the material benefits of the relationship was really worth the trouble.

At length Murdoch spied a possible sanctuary and made a bee-line for the safe haven, using the wrecking ball on the front of the cab to good use as he crashed through a crumbling Victorian brick wall, alarming the cornucopia of residents on the other side. The vehicle passed through with difficulty, the wheels catching on the resultant pile of bricks throwing him out of the cab. Despite the shock he retained the survival instructs to scramble towards the nearest shelter - a tight space underneath a large over-hanging rock. Murdoch hid and for the first time in what seemed like hours it was now eerily quiet as he even became aware of his own very rapid breathing.

The silence was soon broken as in the distance the unmistakable booming footfalls of the giant could be heard coming nearer and nearer. He stared out of the small opening in the ruined wall in petrified anticipation of seeing the giant looming large over the top of the enclosure where he now found refuge. However, as he focused on the horizon, something much nearer encroached on his vision from the top of his field of view. It was an upside down face that gradually waned into focus from above the rock. First, whiskers appeared, then eyes, then the full furry head of an inquisitive and somewhat surprised and perplexed mountain lion. In his haste to escape one predator, Murdoch had inadvertently put himself in mortal danger from another when he had unfortunately bundled into the lion enclosure of Bristol Zoo. The lion, which had been snoozing peacefully on his favourite rock, had been rudely awoken by a noisy yellow beast that had crashed through the tough glass of its home. The beast then appeared to die but only after if released a small man from within it who then scuttled underneath his rock. Neither the lion nor Murdoch had time to enact the age old chase of predator and prey as they were both distracted by the much larger foe of the giant stepping over the smashed wall surrounding the zoo and into the nearby herbaceous border and therefore immediately usurping the lion in the food chain.

13

Reverend Herbert Gooding dabbed his furrowed brow as he stared up at the heavens to see swifts swirling overhead like circus acrobats, swinging on invisible ropes in a sky as blue as the cornflowers that were sprinkled around the graves at his feet. However, this man of the cloth was not craning his neck for this natural spectacle of aviation or indeed even in prayer to the 'big man' upstairs. Herbert's focus of attention fell on something much closer to the ground and indeed getting nearer to the ground every day.

The famous steeple that crowned the church in Steeple Hill was once a magnificent example of Victorian marksmanship. From its tip, virtually the whole of Bristol could be spied and its power and status as the focal point of the parish was there for all to see. Alas now the spire was in a state of great disrepair and the very nature of its striking slender profile was soon to be its downfall as it crumbled and now leaned over to the south like a listing ship about to take its final dramatic descent. Of course the recent earthquakes that had gently shaken the area had only exacerbated the fragile state of the stone needle - small chunks of masonry had already sporadically begun to fall from its great height, endangering the worshippers below each Sunday morning. So far only the elderly gravedigger Alfred had been struck by the falling stonework but luckily he had not been badly harmed. (Although the knock on the bonce he received from the projectile did result in the unstable old man losing his footing one morning and stumbling into the half-dug grave of the local butcher who had sadly passed on not a few days before. Old Alfred had been knocked out cold and his prone form lying in the grave was quite a shock to the gathering funeral party the next morning - especially as, at a glance, Alfred bore an uncanny resemblance to the late sausage stuffer who was the intended for the plot.)

Indeed, unless there was a timely miracle from the messiah himself, the church would surely have to close. Congregations had been dwindling for years and there was no money to repair the old neglected house of God. The thought of the impending decertification of the church made Herbert's brow furrow further until it resembled the deeply ploughed field opposite the churchyard. He was too old now to be shunted to another parish meaning there would be only one option left open to him. It was a choice that filled him with terror...namely retirement and, as a horrific consequence, more time spent with Mrs. Gooding.

Although Herbert was the spiritual leader of the parish and a veritable figure of respect and authority to his parishioners, the reverse was true in the less than sacred place that he called his home. Beatrice Gooding, his dear lady wife, was in complete command of that domain and by goodness, didn't she let him know it. Barely a moment passed when he was not criticised for either not doing something, doing something too much or simply being in the way when she was trying to do something. Somehow he had become an impediment in the life of his wife, something that had to be controlled and organised like a child or, more accurately, an old misplaced and unloved piece of furniture. Any equality and love in the marriage had long since evaporated away like so much leftover communion wine. He had thought of leaving her but he knew she would find a way to make him stay as she appeared to enjoy controlling him.

In truth, despite his stirring sermons from the pulpit full of biblical fire and brimstone, Herbert was a weak-willed man. But now, as the daily remonstrations from 'her indoors' intensified in both vehemence and frequency, pushing him to the very precipice of insanity, he forced himself to summon what little mental strength he still possessed lest he succumb to her desire to shove his fragile mind into a blazing hell of madness.

Beatrice was not a very religious woman and that had troubled him when they had started courting many years ago but despite the obstacle of a lack of shared faith, he soon found he was unavoidably attracted to her. Perhaps he thought he could change her and eventually show her the right path to God but in truth he never knew for sure what had lured him.

Over the years he had gradually learned to live with his wife's lack of faith. Although she belittled and emancipated him at home he found comfort in his church. Here at least was still a confident man who was looked up to for guidance and leadership. Here was his refuge, not just twice on a Sunday but whenever he could squirm away from underneath her stifling grip on his life.

Then suddenly, last Sunday morning during one of his most rousing depictions of the downfall of Sodom and Gomorrah, he spied a shadowy figure in the very last pew at the back of the nave. The eyes from the silhouetted figure bore into him and despite the blinding light that flooded in from the stained glass windows of the east wing he could easily discern the familiar lumpy outline of his wife. She was sitting in the back of the church, his church, after all this time! With the shock he stumbled over the words of his sermon, knocking over his glass of water and sending it tumbling to the stone floor below. Half of the dozen or so stalwarts who still attended every week gasped, thinking this was a dramatic effect to enhance the foreboding tale. The other half jumped as they were rudely awoken from their morning slumber before they went to the pub for a pint and a roast dinner.

That morning she had entered his sanctuary and things would never be the same again. It was not that she had 'seen the light' and found God. Oh no, he knew as soon as he clapped eyes on her that fateful morn that her strangling grip on his life was tightening for the final death throws. There she sat, mentally unsettling him as her thighs spread out along the pew like settling wet clay on a dormant potter's wheel.

His wife entering his final bastion was the final straw and he would not be able to continue under her evil gaze. That morning he stepped down from the pulpit and snuck out the back to his vestry without saying another word, leaving the whole congregation stunned before the flustered organ player plumped her blue rinse and struck up the hymn that signalled the end of the service many, many minutes early.

14

Every day was normally always the same for the solitary male lion at Bristol zoo. It was a regular cycle of feeding and sleeping, against a backdrop of a stream of mocking human visitors who would roar at him from behind the protective Perspex. It was a tedious but admittedly comfortable life and that was the way he had grown to like it. Today however, was turning out to be a very different one from the norm.

The giant of the jungle had been roused by a bumbling object bursting into his enclosure but before he could even get used to this unwelcome intrusion, a creature of a size he had never seen before had stepped over the wall and into the grounds of the zoo. The lion usually had very little if anything to fear and so, with his feline inquisitiveness very much getting the better of him, he slowly padded out to take a better look.

What the lion saw as he first ventured out was not the huge beast but the other familiar fauna of the zoo although their behaviour was now *far* from familiar as they were all exhibiting varying degrees of hysteria. Each creature was enacting their own specific inherent 'fright or flight' mechanism depending on what species they might be. Birds and bats flapped furiously in their cages, unable to break through wire fencing or tough netting. Prairie dogs and meerkats abandoned their look-out posts, raising the alarm in a high-pitched shrill before disappearing into their burrows. Penguins waddled off into regimented lines, flinging themselves into the water or hiding inside their wooden shelters. Primates swung well away on their ropes shrieking and howling as the ostriches predictably buried their heads in the sand. Only the reptiles and the insects made no noticeable movements, either being nocturnal, too small or simply too dim to be concerned by the new arrival that was several hundred or even several thousand times their size.

The human visitors were the last to find refuge, their supposed superior intelligence over the rest of the animal kingdom meaning many took longer to decide which way to escape. Despite their relative sluggishness, it was only a matter of seconds before they too had all scarpered and no higher life forms of any description could be spied in the zoo. The only exceptions to this rule were the perplexed male mountain lion and one ruffled young man in unfashionable clothing.

Lance Murdoch was that last man left in the zoo, now trapped at the back of an enclosure with his only escape route blocked by a huge giant as a lion prowled out of sight somewhere close by. He admitted to himself that he could think of many better places to be at that moment.

He needed a plan and fast. Murdoch looked around for any possible help or inspiration, (which is not easy when you have a huge lion with big teeth in the near vicinity.) He scanned his immediate surroundings. The place appeared to be deserted apart from the giant who worryingly now appeared to be hungry as it could be seen ripping the roof the café in search of food he clearly could smell within. As Murdoch watched the giant tear off the metal canteen roof like a child peeling the lid from a yoghurt pot, he caught a movement in the corner of his eye. Bravely taking his gaze from the giant for a second he peered in the direction of whatever was stirring. The movement was coming from the monkey enclosure where some of the primates had decided the giant posed little threat at the moment and they had ventured back out to swing happily again on their ropes and vines.

Suddenly a spark of cognition ignited in Murdoch's brain. Of course! The monkeys! The idea came to him in a flash of inspiration and he set to work immediately. He glanced quickly in the direction of the giant to ensure his he was still busy pilfering the overpriced café before delving into his pockets to retrieve a huge mobile phone. Murdoch selected a loud ring tone to play before throwing it as far as he could over his shoulder and out of the lion enclosure. The lion growled instinctively and leapt adeptly towards the annoying sound. Murdoch sprang from his hiding place and into his trusty stolen demolition crane. Not daring to look behind him to see if either beast (jungle or folklore) may have spotted him, he turned the keys and prayed.

He breathed a sigh of relief as it sprang noisily into life, spewing dirty diesel fumes behind it. The lion was startled by the new noise but luckily he was still trying to stop the annoying ring-tone on the ancient mobile phone by mauling it to death. Murdoch knew the lion would probably be distracted for quite some time as the old phones were practically indestructible by design but not wanting to hang around to test the theory he sped off, reaching a dizzying speed of at least 10 mph as he gratefully left the king of the jungle behind. Back out in the open ground of the zoo, knowing he did not have the velocity to outpace the giant, he ignored the nearest exit signs and instead headed for the primate zone to execute the next phase of his cunning plan.

Now hidden from the giant beast behind a wall, he was able to put his hastily arranged scheme in place. Daring to leave the protection of his vehicle briefly, he entered the back of the monkey house, quickly finding the food stocks of the hairy swingers. Plundering the stores, he left with purloined handfuls of the monkeys' favourite food - ripe yellow bananas. He hastily tied the bananas at intervals on a long length of rope that was coiled up in a corner. Next Murdoch rattled the cages and enclosures to get the attention of the apes. This was not a difficult task as many of the hairy creatures had not been fed before the chaos had ensued and were delighted to see an animated (if oddly dressed) man pointing to some ripe bananas. Murdoch's hirsute appearance also helped with many of the gorillas thinking he could well be one of their kin with such a hairy chest. (They were not to know the manly chest follicles that carpeted his upper body where actually purchased from a local joke shop.)

Murdoch nearly had all of the elements of his plan in place when the ground shook violently and a huge eye appeared through the doorway of the enclosure, closely followed by a deafening roar. Ignoring his fear he called over one of the main attractions of the zoo, the huge silver-back gorilla named George. Its enormous curved back was turned away from him but soon it shuffled its immense bulk as Murdoch continued to shout at it. Once it had swivelled fully around, the young man did something you are told never to do in a zoo – it looked directly into the eyes of the gorilla. Seeing this as a challenge the silver-back bared its teeth and came charging towards

Murdoch who skipped neatly to the side just before the jungle swinger came crashing toward the sturdy reinforced plastic. The transparent barrier was no match for the running bulk of the gorilla as the rigid pane shattered into millions of pieces. The other monkeys soon followed through the hole, the morass of small primates shielding Murdoch from the angry gorilla that was now becoming distracted anyway by all its tree-dwelling cousins circling around him.

Murdoch grabbed the end of the banana-strewn rope and, swallowing hard, bravely ran out towards the owner of the gigantic orb of an eye, knowing full well it was connected to a gigantic head, arms, legs and the rest of the giant. He ran straight underneath the giant's nether regions, the rope trailing him like a tail. The giant swiped with his fist to swat Murdoch from between his legs like an ant but he was too slow and cumbersome, unable to grab the fleeting eighties throwback. Not looking back, Murdoch ran as fast as he could, praying the monkeys would do the rest. Luckily they did not let him down. The frenzied primates tied the giant in knots as dozens of the creatures ran around its legs, each one holding a different part of the rope, as they all trying to grab as many bananas as they possibly could.

Free of the attention of the giant, Murdoch ran back to his wrecking crane and, already for a second time that day, he made good his escape. Careering back through the punctured outer wall and onto the road, he regained his original focus and headed straight towards his mission of revenge, straight towards a certain house in the ancient village of Steeple Hill.

The giant was momentarily angered by his entrapment but eventually he freed himself from the tangle of knots, much to the continued amusement of the monkeys that nimbly swung around him. The other strange irritant in the little machine had gone but the giant did not care when he caught an unmistakeable movement in the corner of his eye. It was what, or rather whom he had been looking for all along – his brother, in the distance, frolicking in the valley a few miles to the south and east. The giant roared and headed in his direction, his mighty bellow already gaining the attention of his sibling who stared back coldly, his huge eyes clearly visible over the few short miles that separated them.

15

Julia Bradfield hated working for big multi-national companies but she had to admit the money they provided for senior scientific researchers like herself was too good to ignore. She had to admit to herself (although rarely to others due to shame) that her work ethics were being severely tested with her latest commission though. A well known tea company had given her and her team hundreds of thousands of pounds (not to mention new state of the art equipment) to study the effects of large volumes of tea drinking. The company had seen a drop in sales over the last few months after yet another study had linked aluminium deposits naturally found in tea leaves with a higher risk of Alzheimer's in old age. After she accepted the research contract, a representative of the company (in the guise of sharply dressed but forceful men who visited her last month) wanted her work to show that there were no such health issues with their particular brand of tea or else there would be certain 'unpalatable consequences'. Julia was not one to scare easily and rebuffed their vague threat, stressing that her findings would be honest and disliked any suggestion that she might have to 'tweak' her results to give the company the all-important positive sound-bite they so obviously desired.

Julia soon discovered her initial findings would not please the tea company. She had been placing strong tea in the drinking bottles that fed her groups of test mice for some weeks now. The volumes were small but it replicated an average human drinking at least 30 cups of tea a day for a period of 20 years. In the first few weeks the mice acted normally but in the last few days some of them had started to exhibit a rather worrying trait. She would have to put this in her final report but was confident that the tea company would not be concerned. She confidently reasoned that no human could be affected in the same way as nobody could drink the amounts of tea that would result in such a dramatic change.

The good reverend of the village of Steeple Hill was not immune to the burgeoning chaos around him. In fact, he was acutely aware of the maelstrom in the centre of city that was nestled in the valley below. The strains of panic emanating from stricken city dwellers were clearly audible as they drifted up the hillside to the lofty position of the village, carried on the gentle southerly breeze. Despite the din he tried to ignore the increasing cacophony of sirens, screeching tyres and helicopters flying nearby as the holy man had enough of his own problems to deal with and he decided it was time for him to be selfish for once and leave its flock to fend for itself.

At least he was now hatching a plan that may resolve one of his woes. He had realised that the mighty hewn stones that had fallen from the decrepit steeple would make a perfect murder weapon to rid him of his suspicious, scheming, satanic wife. He had the motive, the murder weapon but all that was lacked was a modus operandi and, even more importantly, an alibi. Preferably he also required an outside agent to do the job for him as he doubted he would have the balls to commit such a sinful act himself.

The clergyman paced in the damp grass by the gravestones, flattening and bruising the dry, yellowing blades as he attempted to metaphorically find the missing pieces of the jigsaw that was his uxoricidal plan. Bereft of further ideas, he turned on his heel towards the church, thinking he may find inspiration from one of the gruesome tales explicated in the Old Testament. The shame of using the good book for such devilish means was lost on this man, who had so spectacularly lost his faith.

Herbert stood outside the great door that led back into the permanently chilly interior of the church and paused for a moment, looking upwards. Did he dare send his thoughts heavenwards in the vain hope of divine inspiration or indeed intervention? If he did, would he be struck down and sentenced to an eternal existence of damnation, fire and brimstone? Before he could decide, a possible solution to the missing elements of his deadly problem presented itself noisily and clumsily behind him, busting out of a rabbit hole that blew wide open with the force of a torrent of water and an incongruous and bulky shape. Had his prayers been answered at last?!

'More tea vicar?' said a portly, dishevelled and soaking wet (but clearly very thirsty) Stump as he waggled his (now sadly water-filled) teacups in the direction of the startled holy man.

The rattled clergyman ogled the sturdy newcomer excitedly, seeing immediate potential in the young man. 'Yes, yes of course! You will need to get your strength up after all.' Within what seemed like an impossibly short time interval, the vicar returned with a mug of piping hot tea just as the special duck that mastered the martial arts came out of the tunnel whilst performing an impressive flying kick at nothing in particular.

Stump gratefully accepted his new cup of char, as he wrung the water from his tweed over-garments, delighted to be alive and well after his sodden ordeal.

As Stump contentedly enjoyed his tea, Herbert nervously stooped over the shorter man. 'I...I...I am hoping you are the answer to my prayers!' he stammered bluntly. 'You see I need a strapping young lad to solve a little problem for me.'

'What kind of a problem?' Stump responded with a quizzical air, looking sideways with some curiosity at the taller man as he sipped.

'Well, it involves a woman. My wife to be exact. She is making my existence an utter misery and, to be frank with you, I need her out of my life for once and for all!' screeched Herbert, ending his sentence with a despairing, theatrical flourish of his arms.

'Not really my area of expertise I am afraid,' said the younger man sheepishly, not really following the conversation and wondering if the guy had been supping too much on his communion wine. 'I have to say I am not all that comfortable talking to members of the opposite gender. I guess that all started when my mother left...' Stump tailed off as he again saw visions of a long time ago, of his childhood and his mother leaving, the talks his father used to give him, about what was expected of him....Of course! His mission! How could he have forgotten for so long? Maybe it was meant to be this way, the memories not coalescing in his mind until he was of a certain age, or triggered by a request to aid a helpless and hen-pecked man like the one that now stood above him this very moment. It all made sense to him now. The visions he had been experiencing were not dreams but actually suppressed memories of the teachings his father gave him when he was a young sprat of a lad, the instructions to carry out his bidding to rid the world of modern women and inform them of their true worth, putting them back into place…namely the kitchen!

Silently Stump clenched his fist as he now realised what he was here to do. And where better place to start than with this belittled priest!

The vicar stood back a step as he watched on with a bedazzled air. The young man who he was hoping to enlist to rid him of his other half had fallen eerily quiet. He was about to ask the adolescent if he was alright when the youth began what could only be described as a dramatic and rapid physical metamorphosis.

Stump was already a stocky fellow but suddenly his muscles started to swell even more. His arms began to bulge, filling the sleeves of his tweed jacket like a set of bagpipes being inflated by a gargantuan caber tosser. The coarse coat burst open at the seams to reveal his new rippling biceps and from the sky a small red orb emerged, Stump catching the cricket ball one-handed with great agility as he jumped to his right. Finally from his pocket he produced his pipe and a flat cap that he carefully wedged onto his head. His transformation concluded, he stood there with one mighty hand on his hip, the other looping the ball a few inches into the air and catching it again with a satisfying slap.

'Let us begin,' he said, his voice noticeably deeper and his North Yorkshire accent very much more discernable. He strode towards the great doors and into the church, the priest meekly but excitedly following in his wake as he hurriedly explained the reasons for wanting his wife gone.

16

Alex ended his watery journey by being unceremoniously dumped into a small circular room, thankfully landing softly on a fetid pile of old leaves and other detritus. He gingerly got to his feet, not hiding his revulsion as the stinking material clung to his expensive designer jeans. Embedded in the wall above his head was a small opening, probably just large enough to squeeze through if it wasn't for a robust metal grate covering the aperture. The only other exit appeared to be the tunnel he had just slid out of that ended directly above his head in the ceiling of the structure. Alex attempted to climb the wall, heading for the grated vent but the vertical brick walls covered in wet moss provided precious little in the way of grip. He tried to shout for help, directing his yelps upwards at the barred gap in the wall but after a few minutes all he had achieved was a sore throat and no chilled sauvignon at hand to soothe it.

Before he could despair further at his situation, a small dark shape emerged from the ceiling-top hole. His hope of escape was thus raised but then all but extinguished when he realised it was merely one of the ducks that had followed his watery path. He waited a moment, allowing the bird to ruffle its feathers and rid itself of the fearsome glop it had landed in before he addressed the animal.

'So which one are you?' he asked scornfully.

'I am Donal', replied the duck, avoiding eye contact as he finished preening. 'The magician', it added proudly as it craned its neck to view its companion.

'Ah yes, the one with the name of a knocked-off Irish cartoon character. So, then Donal, I assume you can magic us out of this hole then?' Alex said, with more than a hint of scepticism.

'I'm afraid not my friend. My skills are more centred around illusion and subterfuge. I have to admit they amount to little more than parlour tricks. Good parlour tricks mind, but parlour tricks all the same.' As if to illustrate the point, the duck opened its wings to reveal two bunches of fake flowers. 'And If you were relying on me to fly up to the grate to quack for help, I am sorry but I can't help you in that way either. Alas my wings are not equipped for flying anymore after living underground in such cramped conditions for so long. Therefore the responsibility to extricate ourselves from this hole will have to be solely yours.'

'And how exactly do you suppose I do that? Blow a hole in the wall for us to escape through?'

'Well that would do it, yes!'

'You must be as crazy as you look duck. If we were anywhere else but here I would already be thinking about which sauce to complement your perfectly cooked body with if I hadn't sold you as a curiosity to science or, more likely, the next travelling circus that had rolled through town!'

The duck breathed in slowly through the nostrils positioned high on its beak, attempting to keep its patience. 'Alex, I have some skills but I am here to help you use your own skills.'

'What good is that here? There is nobody around that I can persuade to help us out and all I can move with my mind is a few small stones. How in the name of Giorgio Armani can that help?'

'You are thinking too literally Alex. You need to think outside the box my well-dressed young friend, or at least outside this cell.' Clearly this was not the time for attempted humour so Donal cleared his raspy throat to clarify. '*Who* or *what* do you have a special connection with to call on in your hour of need?'

The question made Alex think deeply and reflect on his life. He realised that most of his best relationships were with inanimate objects, finding them often more beautiful and trustworthy than people. For example, he considered the gentle curve on a bottle of wine or a vase made from Bristol Blue glass more aesthetically pleasing than many of the female form he had encountered. As for whom or what to trust when he needed help, he knew he would choose fine German automobile engineering over the unpredictable nature of people any time.

Therefore in the end he could think of only one true answer to the duck's strange enquiry. 'Do you mean my car?' Alex proposed.

'Yes, your car!' shrieked the duck. 'Close your eyes and think of it now, think of where it is, sitting patiently outside your house and imagine it starting up and driving itself to you.'

Despite the absurdity of the situation, Alex closed his eyes and concentrated. It was easy to see his car sitting on the roadside, parked at a gentle tilt with two wheels on the pavement, ready and waiting to be used by its owner. He imagined sitting in the bucket seat and turning the ignition. He could see the coloured lights on the dashboard illuminating and the engine sparking magically into life. But then, the image of the car evaporated. 'Oh, this is preposterous. This isn't going to work. How can my car find me?!' grumbled Alex after he lost his focus and then his temper, petulantly kicking at the leaf litter without a thought for his shoe leather.

'Please, try once more. It will know,' the duck implored, locking eye contact with the young man who towered above him in the dim light. 'It may be the only way we can get out of here in time.'

Alex stared back with incredulity at the duck but for some reason he found himself sighing before closing his eyes once more. After all, he wanted to believe he could have the power to command any objects at will, even those he could not see.

He took a deep breath, regaining his concentration. His car materialised again in his mind's eye, sleek and shiny after a recent wash and polish. He imagined opening the low door and ducking to ensure his expensive shades perched on the top of his head did not get scratched as he lowered himself into the padded and internally heated seat. He turned the key in the ignition, half-way for the electrics to respond with a quiet melody of beeps and electronic whirrs before he turned the metal probe fully, hearing the engine roar into life as the needles swayed gracefully into their correct positions on the dials. Checking the mirrors he pulled out, starting his imaginary drive. The duck watched on closely to ensure he kept his concentration, almost amused as he saw Alex hold an imaginary wheel in front of him and press his feet into the decaying leaves, just where the pedals would be.

A few hundred yards away, outside an average looking semi-detached house in Steeple Hill, a car gently pulled away from its position on the kerb-side, gradually gaining speed as it headed off down the road. An elderly couple walking their dog noticed the expensive and conspicuous car drive off and for a fleeting moment they looked at each other, both unsure whether there was a driver in the front seat. Together they dismissed the silly notion as a trick of the light and their fading eye-sight. They went on with their day, human minds more comfortable to seek a 'normal' solution to confusing visual stimuli.

Before long the sounds in Alex's imagination matched those that could be heard outside, not that he noticed himself. In the real world the car had left the road and turned down a dirt track, occasionally leaping briefly into the air as it took a blatant disregard for the ruts and potholes it came across. The track turned sharply to the right but the car pressed straight on, swerving past large tress as smaller saplings and weeds gently whipped its under-carriage. A few yards further on and the flat ground abruptly ceased, the shiny red beast taking flight, a small escarpment providing a ramp that propelled the vehicle high into the air. With nothing beneath the wheels they span freely as the engine gunned down, a sound that vibrated powerfully within the close confines of a small stone structure just below the heavily polished rotating black circles of rubber.

Alex awoke from his vision and instinctively moved to the back of the confined enclosure just in the nick of time as moments later there was an almighty crash. The wall opposite gave way as something large and red side-swiped the tiny building and came to rest a few yards away, stones of the walled structure bursting inwards from the impact before luckily coming to rest before they struck the soft bodies of man and duck.

Alex and the duck squinted, their eyes taking time to adjust to the light and dust that now flooded into their cell. Gingerly they stepped out of the rubble of the destroyed wall and into a woodland clearing. Alex stared at his pride and joy nearby. It had luckily come to rest upright on its four wheels but it was battered and bruised by its misadventure. At least it still appeared to be mechanically sound as the engine purred away happily in its unfamiliar surroundings.

'Thank goodness you are alright! I do think you are clearly in need of a bit of TLC though', exclaimed Alex.

'Oh, I think I'll be alright,' replied the duck as he put a few stray feathers back in place that had become dislodged when the car had crashed into their temporary prison.

'Not you, you stupid duck. I meant my beloved!' replied Alex as he reached into the boot of his dented car to produce a clean nappy, proceeding to use the baby-soft material to delicately wipe dust off his vehicle with a vigorous but caring fervour.

After the quick polish Alex hopped into his self-entitled two-seater 'babe-magnet', the flightless duck flopping into the passenger seat. (The bird permitted inside the vehicle on the strict proviso that he did not foul the expensive interior furnishings.) Alex turned the ignition and carefully left the green glade, following tracks along the river before gratefully returning to smooth paved roads.

Within a couple of minutes Alex was back home to rest at his rented abode. He thanked himself for having the foresight to chill a bottle of Sauvignon before he left and settled down with a cool glass of the pale liquid in his favourite chair. He had thought it might be fun to practice his new brain power by attempting to pour the glass with the power of his mind but he didn't want to risk spilling any of the precious fluid and ruining the expensive woollen rug at his feet.

Looking out the window as he took his first gulp he could see his beautiful car safely on the road once more. It would require some minor repairs but thumbing through car magazines for the relevant parts was never a chore.

As Alex salivated over potential duck dishes, absently wondering if the talking variety tasted any different to the normal common or garden variety, the object of his culinary desires was mentally stewing downstairs, locked in a cupboard. Alex had found the duck quite annoying since their return, the feathered fool insisting they leave again immediately to find the others and continue the quest. Alex however had decided he needed a little rest. He was sure that if he was alright then his housemates would also be safe and would return soon enough. After turning on his stereo and selecting his favourite Phil Collins tracks he could barely hear the duck downstairs as it banged on the inside of a locked cupboard door in protest. He began to snooze, unsuspecting of whom was about to shatter his respite.

17

The still soaking figure of Jack Stump confidently stormed into the church, darkening the floor with water wherever his heavy feet slopped on the flag-stones. The assembled congregation, (in attendance for their weekly L.I.F.T. (Ladies In Fellowship Together) coffee morning), gasped at the sight of the strapping, rugged youth but Stump did not wait for them to settle after his unexpected arrival, immediately turning his attention to the women who were sat in the battered and gnarled wooden pews.

A lady in her early forties was his first victim but to Stump it was her who was perpetrating the crime. 'You!' he belted raspily in her direction. 'Your skirt is far too short for your age and I hope for your sake that lunch is already prepared otherwise your husband will not be happy when he returns from the golf course.' Ashamed, the middle-aged woman pulled down her skirt as she sat, the material now covering her knees.

Duffy, the duck well versed in martial arts of many kinds, stood by the door preventing any wood-be escapees as Stump moved down the aisle, picking out another unfortunate female to unfurl his wrath on. 'And you! I bet all your children were not from the same father and born out of wedlock to boot. Shame on you, you common harlot!' The middle-aged woman covered her mouth, more due to shock rather than shame.

The transformed Yorkshire enforcer of yesterday's standards moved on to the next row and was just about to vent his considerable anger against womankind on another quaking member of the opposite sex when he heard another more worthy female opponent entering the church behind him, her stiletto heels clearly audible on the stone floor. Her great stature, enhanced by the high heels, cast a long shadow down the centre of the church, the greyness threatening to engulf the haranguing juvenile. He turned to face his latest foe and as he prepared to begin his latest tirade, Herbert emitted a short squeal before cowering behind a pew. Stump rightly guessed from the defensive actions of the vicar that this hag must be the holy man's very own 'trouble and strife'.

'And…as…for…you…!' Stump bellowed in an almost devilish drone.

'Don't start Jack. Just listen to me,' Herbert's wife replied in a calming tone before Stump could say another word. 'There is something you need to know.'

Incandescent with rage at the indignant interruption, Stump recommenced his tirade. 'No, you listen to me my dear woman. I don't know how you know my name but I do know that you have made this poor man's life a misery. You have hounded him from dawn to dusk, never giving him a moment's peace and emasculating him at every turn whilst flagrantly disregarding your wifely duties around the house. He also suspects you of fornicating with another member of his flock. I certainly wouldn't put that past you. In fact…,' continued Stump, enjoying putting a woman twice his age firmly into her place, '…you remind me of someone I knew from my youth.'

'Your mother?'

Stump was shocked that she guessed correctly but he wasn't about to let that put him off his stride. 'What in the name of Yorkshire would you know about me and my mother? Besides, this is about you, not me,' he said defiantly, even if a hint of uncertainty had crept into his northern brogue, perhaps knowing deep down the next words that were going to be uttered from the mouth of this lady.

'Jack. It's not about me, or you. It's about *us* because Jack. I am your mother.'

18

Hannah abruptly reached the end of her watery slide as her derriere slammed against a large steel grill. The water travelled on where she could not – through the gaps in the grate and under a walkway before re-emerging at the head of a man-made waterfall the other side. She peered out between the metal bars and was able to see she was now at street level. Although that was about all she could elucidate as her field of vision was restricted. Throngs of legs filed past her at a fast pace, all their owners heading in the same direction on the pavement directly in front of her.

She could sense the atmosphere was one amounting to mild panic and deduced one of the giants must have been spotted nearby but probably too far away to cause real terror as people were not screaming or running at full pelt.

Hannah strained to look beyond the weaving jungle of trousers, skirts and shoes, following the flow of the water as it was channelled and piped to form fountains, water-spouts and gentle cascades. Youths often made good use of the fast-flowing clean water to paddle and play whereas their older brothers and sisters entertained themselves by adding detergent to the shallow pools, creating clouds of foam that would build up like flotsam before being torn apart by the breeze, floating away in irregular clumps.

She watched as the last of the frolicking youngsters were scooped up by parents and carers like rag-dolls, most of them protesting, not understanding the fear of their elders. Her voyeurism was curtailed when something small banged against her feet. Startled, she jumped away but soon relaxed when she saw it was one of the ducks from the cavern that had been swept along with her. The duck stretched out and ruffled its feathers in sequence from head to tail before improbably producing a pair of spectacles from under its plump feathers and perching them delicately on its beak.

'I am guessing you are the intelligent one?' proffered Hannah.

If the duck had eyebrows he certainly would have raised them. 'Statistically that would be the case, compared to humans and most definitely compared to other ducks,' he said proudly before plucking a loose feather to wipe the lenses of his glasses.

'Maybe you can use your intelligence to get us out of here then?'

The duck shook its head vigorously. 'That my dear, will I'm afraid be down to you. I may be intelligent but in this very particular circumstance I can only work out the best way to escape. I calculate that the highest probability of us continuing safely on our way is related to us seeking aid from an external source.'

'You mean I need to call for help? Is there nothing we can do by ourselves?'

The duck looked at Hannah blankly. 'My dear girl, despite all your education you still fail to grasp that you cannot do everything by yourself. Sometimes you need the assistance of others, we all do. It is our best chance of getting out of here quickly. However even my proposed strategy has only around a 24.3% chance of success.'

Hannah thought about what the duck was saying. The company of others was something that she always rejected whenever possible, due to a combination of shyness and sheer disgust at the way the vast majority of people thought and acted. She had already been forced to enlist the help of her housemates today which had been difficult enough. Asking for help from strangers would be another kettle of fish entirely.

But the timid and fiercely self-sufficient young lady knew deep down that in this particular situation there was no real alternative. After steeling herself she called out through the grate for help. However her inhibitions resulted in a feeble vocal attempt that was easily drowned out when it reached the boisterous hullabaloo outside. The duck rolled his eyes, waddled over and promptly bit Hannah's exposed ankles as hard as he could muster. (Despite the evolutionary disadvantage of lacking teeth, it was able to exert a considerable vice-like grip.) Hannah let out an eye-watering scream that was noticed by many fleeing the scene outside although not that many of them knew, or more importantly cared, from where the ululation had originated.

She waited a few seconds for a response from the passers-by. When nobody bent down to look, the duck prepared to administer a second bite on the now sore ankle but it stopped just as it had opened its jaw to its full extension as they both saw something moving straight towards them from beyond the grate, perpendicular to the running crowds. At first Hannah only caught glimpses of what looked like a predator stalking her, using the thundering herds for cover as they scattered. But then she saw more and more of the slow moving beast until without warning a giant black orb came crashing towards the metal grill between them. Both woman and duck retreated just in time as the wrecking ball bent the metal rods back as if they were made of molten toffee. Hannah rushed out to gratefully embrace her knight in shining armour, fully prepared to exhibit a rare show of unbridled affection for her saviour. She wondered who had helped to free her, this normally staunchly self-reliant woman who had been reduced to a reluctant damsel in distress. Now outside, she stopped in her tracks when she saw who had liberated her from her predicament.

Hannah reluctantly climbed into the vehicle, next to her 'saviour' who greeted her with a wry smile, seemingly pleased at whom this 'damsel in distress' had turned out to be. She cursed her misfortune that the one person who happened to pass at the right moment and had opted to free her in her hour of need was her landlord!

'Fancy meeting you here!' he said ironically.

'Can we just get out of here please?' replied Hannah, trying not to make eye with the character seated to her left, feeling like a schoolgirl being driven home by the headmaster.

'Absolutely.'

'Great.'

'On one condition.'

'What?!' said an exasperated Hannah, abruptly losing her cool as she spied one of the giants appearing from behind a nearby building.

'On the condition that we go back to my house to collect all the rent that I am owed. Especially from that urchin Alex!'

'Perfect!' muttered a squirming Hannah, crossing her arms casually in a surly manner, hoping that he would now stop talking and just get a move on. After all, she needed to get back to Steeple Hill to be able to deal with the giants. She decided to worry about the issue of overdue rent when they were safely back in the village.

Unseen by its two occupants, the forgotten 'clever' duck hopped onto the roof of the vehicle, just as the lumbering beast pulled away at its languid top speed. In the distance one of the giants loomed large in the skyline behind them but never came close, seemingly content with its continued destruction of the city centre, venting its rage on inanimate buildings until it could find its brother.

The unlikely trio soon lost sight of the gargantuan menace as they made slow but steady progress along the winding zigzag streets of Bristol's contrasting districts and towards the old village of Steeple Hill.

A few minutes of bone-jarring travelling later, they arrived back in the village. The landlord slowed to park on the roadside as they approached the house but Hannah leapt out just before they stopped, risking minor injury but gaining valuable seconds before he could follow her. She ran to the garden gate just as the landlord's vehicle came to rest, the driver carelessly bumping a parked car into the road, much to the chagrin of the mothers who struggled to get past the new obstruction as they drove to the nearby private school in their 'all-terrain' vehicles (that were only ever driven on tarmac) to pick up their little darlings.

Hannah bounded up to the front door and reached through a throng of dangling ivy to pull on a concealed chain. Inside the house, a bell chimed at an ear-splitting volume.

Upstairs Alex jumped up from his comfortable chair where he had been enjoying his afternoon siesta. Despite sleeping and the sudden shock of the alarm, he had somehow managed not to spill a drop of wine from the crystal glass he still held in his hand. He knew the sound of that alarm well. The housemates used it as an early warning system for unwanted guests and he set about his well-rehearsed tasks post haste!

106

Alex did not have to worry about his own room (that was always in an immaculate condition) so he turned his attention to the rest of the house. Outside his room on the wall was what looked like a humble light switch. Alex quickly pressed it with a click. He waited anxiously and for a moment nothing happened but then to his relief whirrings and rumblings began to be heard all over the semi-detached building. Pressing the switch had brought to life a contraption devised by man (or Stump in this case) of such cunning and guile it was a true wonder to behold. In the kitchen strong magnets hidden in the walls buzzed into life, propelling metal cutlery through the air from wherever they laid abandoned to land neatly into the open dishwasher. Dirty crockery on worktops were mechanically slid out of view into secret cubby-holes and the floor was washed and dried in seconds with an elaborate system employing an array of sprinklers and hair-dryers that popped out from behind false wall adornments. In the other rooms, carpets were cleaned by pre-programmed automated vacuum cleaners that knew the layout of the room without being guided. Finally, any dirty clothes and dirtier magazines were swept under beds by giant robotic blades that resembled windscreen wipers as they traversed each room in synchrony.

Outside the front door, Hannah was in the midst of a coughing fit as she tried to cover the noise of the machinery that was sanitising the house inside. Naturally the landlord was growing restless. 'Do you not have your keys Hannah?'

'Um, no…that's why I rang the bell,' she said with a nervous grin, trying not to envisage the state of the house before she left. (Hannah hated having to pander to this distasteful man but she knew they all had to keep him sweet as the total sum of their overdue rent was not an inconsequential matter).

'Well, I am sure I have my landlord's set somewhere,' Murdoch said as he began to root around in his leather 'man-bag' that, in his eyes, was definitely not a handbag…regardless of where it may have been originally purchased.

Before he could find his keys, Hannah was given the 'green light' from Alex. (This was literally a green light in the form of a fake flower by the door that shone green when the house was ready). Now relaxed to a degree she opened the door to take control of the unscheduled visit.

As the landlord and tenant crossed the threshold, the air that wafted out from the interior was light and inviting with a whiff of rose petals and camomile. Freshly brewed coffee could also be detected as a bass note on the olfactory system, the smells mixing pleasingly to generate the perfume of an ideal home.

Hannah had made sure she barged through the front door first, just in case, but she quickly realised she had no cause for concern. She breathed a sigh of relief as the house almost audibly sparkled from floor to ceiling. Only a lonely hairdryer dangled preciously as it swung above the kitchen floor, entangled in its lead that had prevented it from being reeled back into its hiding place. She was even more relieved to see Alex again, safe and well as he majestically glided down the stairs like a modern-day Noel Coward.

Earlier, when Alex had arrived back home, he had retired into more comfortable attire – specifically his velvet smoking jacket and slippers with cushioned lamb's wool lining - and it was in these threads in which he now proceeded in interlocution with the landlord. Hannah scurried off unnoticed, leaving her housemate to engage in the social not-so-niceties of a conversation between debtor and collector.

The landlord addressed the well dressed man. 'Ah, Mr…Wall,' he said, pretending snootily to momentarily forget his name. 'It has been a while. We seem to keep…missing each other!'

'Indeed we do. A most unfortunate pattern of coincidences.' said Alex coolly, seemingly more interested in inspecting his manicured fingernails than the rather forced conversation.

'Or more exactly, your rent and that of your housemates…' (he glanced left and right in almost pantomime fashion, as if expecting to see the other two residents cowering behind the coffee table), '…seems to keep missing my bank account!'

'Now I don't think that is strictly true is it Mr. Murdoch…' replied Alex with hands clasped behind his back, '…we all give you cheques once a month.'

'I apologise, that is indeed true and there would be no issue if these cheques did not have rubber bands attached!'

'I am not sure I know to what you are referring Mr. Murdoch.'

'They bounce Mr. Wall. The cheques all bounce!'

Alex looked his landlord straight in the eyes for the first time and almost whispered 'I don't think that is really going to be a problem though, is it Mr. Murdoch?'

Murdoch's expression changed from one of frustration to one of complete calm in an instant. 'I…I…think you are right Mr. Wall. I don't think it will be a problem at all. Please, just pay me when you can. No interest to be charged obviously. I won't disturb you any longer.' Alex smiled as Murdoch turned away and left the house in peace, closing the door quietly behind him.

But then, just before the landlord reached the front gate, he paused and shook his head wildly. Cleared from the temporary grogginess of the hypnosis, he turned back, making a defiant return up the garden path. Alex's face dropped as he watched forlornly through the lounge window.

Not waiting for permission to enter this time, Murdoch flung the door open to address his despondent tenant. 'No, not this time. You are *not* going to control me again! Now it is my turn but first I must tell you the main reason for my visit. Yes, I came here for my rent but more important than that, I came for revenge after what you have done to me all these years.'

Alex was genuinely shocked, bemused and a little amused. 'What *I* have done to *you*? I had not met you before you became our landlord!'

'That could not be further from the truth, Mr. Wall…or should I say…my dearest brother Alex!'

For the second time in a few moments the smile was wiped from Alex's face. This time though his happy demeanour would not return as the revelation was accompanied by a swift right hook from Murdoch that he had not seen coming. The haymaker connected soundly with Alex's chin, sending him crashing to the floor.

19

An uneasy standoff was now being played out in the crumbling church as Jack Stump stood facing a woman who purported to be his estranged bearer into this world – his long lost mother. The once startled congregation looked on, now enthralled as if they were watching an afternoon 'made for television' drama film.

Stump moved from his mark and stormed past his mother and headed for the doorway to the churchyard, not willing to give her even the time of day.

'Won't you at least let me explain? I haven't seen you for nearly 30 years!' pleaded the former Mrs. Stump.

'And whose fault is that exactly?' replied Jack, turning to face her again just as he reached the gaping doorway. 'Assuming you really are my mother of course.'

'Its not what you think,' she said, emotion now evident in her voice. 'I suspect your father told you I ran away with another man. Is that right?'

Her son didn't move a muscle.

'Well, it wasn't true. In fact it was the opposite of the truth as it was your father who was having an affair!' The congregation gasped collectively. 'He was seeing another woman for years. I put up with it at first for the sake of the family but in the end I could not stand it anymore so I left. Of course, there is nothing I wanted more than to take you with me but if I did I knew he would hunt us down and never let us settle together. I knew his parents, your paternal grandparents were rich and I thought he would go to them for money and they would help him look after you financially and give you the best future possible. By the looks of you though I was wrong. He obviously didn't do that and I truly hope you didn't grow up wanting for anything.

'When I left I drifted from town to town for a while, picking up work doing cleaning jobs or bar work. Then, one day, I saw people recruiting for the army. I enlisted immediately, at the time not really knowing why but I think now I wanted to do something your father would disapprove of me, a woman, doing more than anything else.

'After a few years I happened to be stationed near here and it became my home when I left the army. By chance I found Herbert, a good, safe man. I guess I was drawn to him as he is the complete opposite of your father.

'Jack, I have always struggled to live with what I did and whether it was the right choice or not. It was the most difficult decision of my life, leaving my only son, but I had to do what I thought was best for you. I never forgot you though – you were on my mind every day and whenever I saw a child of your age I wondered if they looked like you. It ate me up inside not being with you and in recent years I probably took all that mental anguish out on poor Herbert and I am deeply sorry for that too.' Hand on her chest she turned to look at her beleaguered other half. Herbert could not bear to return her gaze.

'Call it coincidence or fate if you like but you followed me here to this very village. I first saw you a few months ago and I could not be sure it was you Jack but in my heart I knew it was. I'm afraid you are the spitting image of your father from his younger days when we were courting. After I saw you that first time I thought you must be a student here so I made enquiries at the university and they confirmed it was you. They did say you were almost a stranger when it came to the lecture hall but we can talk about that another time!

'Anyway, I struggled to decide what to do, how to approach you and what to say. Recently I even started coming here to the church to seek guidance from the almighty even though I cannot normally abide religious places.'

She paused before realising she also needed to address her husband too.

'My dear Herbert. I know I also need to apologise to you properly. I have acted abominably lately but you have to try to understand that when I saw my little boy again my life unravelled before my eyes. All my thoughts turned to him and I had no time for anything else in my life, including you.'

Herbert shrugged dismissively, anger still etched in his features.

It was Jack who found the strength to respond. 'You are lying!' he shouted. 'My father and I never had a penny. He built our home from rocks with his own bare hands and laboured all his working life. Any little money he had he used to buy my clothes, bus fares for college and, most importantly, new cricket bats. And we never heard from you, not once in all these years.

'Oh Jack, I wrote to you every month, sending cheques in every letter. It wasn't much but I sent what I could.'

'Utter rubbish, woman! I never got so much as a dirty penny from you. You are not my mother, just some stupid adulterous woman who may genetically be my mother but in reality you are nothing to me.'

Jack turned away for a final time but he was nearly knocked from his triumphant striding by the most powerful tremor yet, one that rained down stonework outside the stained-glassed windows. It sounded like the steeple had collapsed from the church itself.

Desperate to get through to Stump, his mother continued. 'You never received anything? Not even any of the tea bags?'

'Teabags?' shouted Jack with incredulity. 'Teabags...' he repeated more reflectively, searching his mind's eye and examining the mug he still held as if that would hold the answer.

'Yes, teabags!' His mother was at last buoyed. She sensed a hint of recognition in the face of her only offspring. 'Everywhere I travelled in the army I sent you a box of teabags from where I was stationed. At first I sent you normal letters, hoping beyond hope that you would see them and maybe, one day forgive me enough to respond. But after a while I knew there was no point in sending any more. Your father never responded to me so I was sure he had not been reading them to you or let you read them yourself when you were old enough. So I devised a plan to send boxes of tea instead. I prayed that your father's love of a cup of char would mean he would use the tea despite the fact I sent it. I wrote hidden messages in each box in tiny writing, small enough to be missed by the incurious eye of an adult but something that I thought may be spotted by a more inquisitive child like your younger self.

I sent Lotus and Jasmine tea from Vietnam, Persimmon and Mugwort tea from Korea, Bubble tea from Taiwan, Sweet tea from the American deep south, Masala chai from India, Rooibos from South Africa and even Tisane from South America. Do you not remember any of this?'

Jack thought back to his childhood, searching deep into his memories. Perhaps something was ringing true about his mother's tale after all. One of his earliest recollections was the smell of tea leaves and how the odour clung to the inside of the white cardboard with the fine brown dust of the small tea particles that had escaped from the teabags in transit. The comforting scent would linger long after the last bag had been used, adhering to the small picture cards that would be also often be contained within. He remembered the unexplained anger of his father as he would rip the colourful boxes into a hundred pieces before chucking the fragments onto the fire. He remembered now though that the frugal nature of his father meant he did not throw away the tea, even if some of the strange brands was not to his tastes.

He could now recall with clarity that he was confused as to why his father would become so irate at the ornate boxes and how he would retrieve un-singed pieces from the fire when his father had dozed off in his chair. He would then lay the small scraps on the floor, trying to piece together the intricate and colourful images and patterns. Sometimes he would indeed spy some truncated, spidery handwriting but, even after he had learnt to read, the messages were all too often too segmented to make any sense. It was rare that a whole message was visible as missives were too often rudely punctuated by the jagged edge where the box had been torn apart in anger. Only once did a complete note appear, written in light blue pen within the curved boundary of a rearing elephant that was majestically painted on a box of tea from somewhere in India. He could see it now as if it was yesterday, all of a sudden after all these years. Stump had now long since forgotten the exact words but it was a powerful missive, a long out-pouring of love and regret from his mum. He could now recall with clarity, as if he could see the note in front of him that she had indeed tried to explain why she had left him and how one day she would return.

How had he forgotten all this until now? Had his father brain-washed him somehow? Indoctrinated him to forget about his mother, feeding him false stories and lies for all these years? Or perhaps his own brain made him forget, the realisation too painful to deal with. Either way, now that mattered not a jot. Back in the present, a toothy smile grew on Jack's face as the big lump ambled towards his mother, huge arms wide open in acceptance.

'Mummy!' he exhaled as he gave the woman a lung-collapsing embrace.

20

Alex awoke with one hell of a headache and for once it wasn't due to his over indulgence from the previous evening involving several bottles of Chablis. It did feel like a hangover though as his mouth felt like dry carpet and his body ached like he had slept for hours in a contorted position. Presently he realised these sensations were hardly surprising as a bit of old carpet had been stuffed in his mouth and he was sat on an old wooden stool in the kitchen of the house, his waist lashed to the uncomfortable seat. He tried to move his arms but those had been tied behind his back. His legs were also tightly bound together at his ankles, the rough twine digging into the thin skin as he wriggled. Looking forewords he saw a blurred white image that gradually coalesced in front of his eyes. It was Murdoch who stood in front of him, looking very different after a change of clothes. He now donned a classic white suit with a black t-shirt underneath, mismatching florescent socks and boat shoes. He looked for all the world like a band member from Duran Duran or perhaps even The Man from Del Monte (minus the Panama hat and passion for high quality fruit.) Murdoch stood still in front of Alex, watching his prone prey as he menacingly bit off the end of a curly wurly chocolate bar.

For the first time Alex could see the family likeness in his features. Maybe he should have noticed before but how many tenants are able to look their landlord in the eye?

Murdoch walked over to a ghetto blaster that now stood on the sideboard. From a shabby pile of cassette tapes he picked one out and placed it in the slot on the top of the oversized music player.

'Can you remember the first album you ever bought Alex? Most people can but I wonder how many lie when asked as they don't want to reveal their embarrassing initial tastes in music.

'I can. I remember my first one vividly. Mum had one of those music catalogues that were all the rage back in those days. One month, after choosing a couple of Eurhythmics albums from the latest pamphlet, she said she had two 'free' choices that she would let us pick. You quickly opted for *Push* by *Bros*, a populist choice you may say. As for me, well I didn't know much about music so I made my decision purely based on the album covers. After perusing the catalogue for quite some time I finally plumped for *Introspective* by the *Pet Shop Boys.'*

Murdoch pressed the chunky play button with a clunk and a click. After a few seconds of laboured whirring, a tinny and muffled 80's electro sound filled the room.

'I knew nothing about their music or their influences but I loved the colourful psychedelic rainbow stripes of the cover depicted in the brochure.

'As soon as it arrived in the post a couple of weeks later I impatiently tore off the cellophane wrapping, opened the transparent housing with a creak and carefully coaxed the small grey cassette tape out. To me it was like taking a prized oyster from its shell. Reverently I placed the tape in my black walkman with a small oval 'bass boost' button and pressed play. (Incidentally I had no idea what the 'bass boost' button did as it seemed to have a negligible effect on the tone of the music. I even thought 'bass' was pronounced like the fish for many years).

'The album itself starts with the song *Left to my own Devices* although the lyrics are preceded by nearly two minutes of a pleasing full orchestral intro sequence that you are currently enjoying. I have to admit that many of the feelings that the words describe were too adult for me to understand at the time. I could not imagine being old enough to drive a car or falling in and out of love but some lines did strike a chord with my fragile young self.'

To Alex's horror, Murdoch began to sing. *'I was a lonely boy, no strength, no joy, a world at the bottom of the garden'.*

Somewhere nearby a dog howled.

'That lonely boy was me, playing in the den behind Dad's stash of bamboo canes behind the garage.

'The second ditty, *I want a dog,* another song about loneliness, also rang true with me. I wanted companionship from a dog when I was a lad but mother never agreed to it. Admittedly I wanted a nice friendly yellow Labrador or Golden Retriever like Bouncer from the Aussie soap opera Neighbours and not a silly little Chihuahua like the song but I could obviously adapt the sentiment to my own situation.

'Next, *Domino Dancing* was more of a *Latin* inspired number. It still had the modern electronic sound but interlaced with a more samba feel, some jaunty piano notes and saxophone undertones not unlike the demo tune on a cheap electric keyboard. A pleasant tune but the meaning I could not juxtapose with my experiences as it was a somewhat bitter retrospective look at a loving relationship that had turned sour through jealousy or infidelity.

'We are now at the midpoint of this short album and the next song, *I'm not Scared,* illustrates a definite turning point, indicating more of a positive outlook. Commencing with a short rousing celebratory marching melody, it switches to a punchy electro-drum beat with rapid see-sawing violin notes. Listening to this song gave me strength to endure my life and give me some hope for the future.'

Murdoch started to warble once more. *'If I was you I wouldn't treat me the way you do. I don't care baby, I'm not scared.'*

'Always in my mind is another fun uplifting song. The varying interwoven beats with frequent key changes are simply pleasing to the ear. The incongruity of the desperate pleading lyrics asking for *just one more chance* somehow does not seem to change the positive, even jokey version of the Elvis Presley classic. The comedic attitude is only reinforced as the song breaks down in the next verse with a full use of voice altering equipment to stretch the vocals from a deep base up to the highest notes and back again before the song rebuilds to an adrenaline rushing celebratory crescendo of drums and fireworks.

'Lastly, *It's Alright* cements the about turn from dark days to light, even starting with a choir delivering the simple mantra of the title with almost religious connotations of salvation. Current worldwide skirmishes are listed followed by a declaration that music is the real saviour for the world. The stabbing notes point at the listener with unceasing repetition, rather like a drunk man angrily drilling his point home.

'I believed that song Alex. I thought the music of the Pet Shop Boys could save the world and that everything would be alright. How wrong I was.'

If Alex hadn't been scared before, he certainly was now.

'At least I am hopeful that last song will shortly come true for me my brother but more about the present and my wonderful future later. First we must discuss the past.

'Ever since you were born you seem to have had some sort of power over me, or more exactly the people around us. In the eyes of everyone you could do no wrong. Any misdemeanour you made was somehow blamed on me. If you broke a pane of glass in the greenhouse, it was my fault. If you spilt a drink on the new carpet, I got the blame. If you forgot to tidy our shared bedroom, somehow it was me who had made the mess. At sport neither of us excelled but even in that field you showed slightly more skill than me, always scoring the late winner in our garden kick-arounds, just as the timer chimed on our Casio digital watches.'

Alex tried to respond but he forgot he could not as he had carpet wedged in his mouth.

'It got worse at school of course!' Murdoch continued. 'When there were no 'A grades' on my report I would get the mother of all tongue lashings but if you got 'B's' and 'C's' you were given praise for trying hard and your hair ruffled as you were sent on your way to play. When I struggled in further education all hell broke loose at home but when you also flopped a couple of years later, you somehow escaped any flak and seemed to be a model student in the eyes of everyone! I never understood how you did that until recently.

'Our parents were ashamed of me compared to the light that shone from you, their golden boy. They told anyone who'd listen about your stellar achievements, especially in the Christmas family letters to relatives where your various triumphs that year were proudly and floridly described on page after page whereas I was relegated to the odd footnote scribbled in the margins as an afterthought.'

Murdoch slowly moved closer to his stricken sibling, never breaking eye-contact until he was inches from Alex's bruised face. 'It's true that you have a special gift Alex. It took me twenty years to realise it but that is why we were treated so differently. I always thought our parents were just more lenient towards you. But no, it's *you* isn't it my dear brother, some power inside of you. That is why I had to leave. That was the only way I would gain control over my life and not have your unnatural influence towering over me, putting me in the shade. I bet mum and dad told you I died whilst travelling didn't they?'

Alex nodded slowly.

'An unfortunate incident involving a llama in Guatemala during my gap year?'

Again, his brother nodded sourly.

'It was a plausible ruse and I wasn't surprised when I heard our parents had pretended I wasn't on this mortal coil any longer. And so I escaped our poisonous family fold but my problems did not end there. You see you left a legacy dear brother. Years of abject failure compared to you and I found it impossible to relate to the modern world and socialise with my peers. For some reason I could only found solace in the decade in which I was most pilloried and struggled at your invisible mental grip...the 1980's.

'I know it must be difficult to comprehend my point of view but, to help explain the mental anguish I have felt over the last couple of decades, I have a neat little analogy to show you.' Murdoch moved towards the sideboard to where he picked up a hammer.

Alex's eyes went wide as he saw the weapon. He shook his head and tried to hop back on the seat he was bound to.

'You see, I have always thought that happiness in life is dependent on four factors. You could think of it as the four legs of a stool, in fact just like the one you are sat on.' Alex looked down frantically at the stool on which he was perched.

'If your stool has all four legs, then, no problem, you have a good stable life! But if, my dear brother, for whatever reason one or more of these legs are taken away from under you then your balance of life suffers. Are you beginning to catch my drift?'

Alex was not sure he did but when faced with a hammer-wielding Pet Shop Boys loving maniac seeking revenge he was hardly going to argue. He nodded furiously in the affirmative.

'I will demonstrate what I mean,' said Murdoch in a crazed tone. 'The first leg in the analogy is friends and family. You see, the company of others has always eluded me, because of how you and our parents didn't want to know me and I became a recluse without the support of a loving family or close confidantes.' Suddenly Murdoch swung his hammer in a low arc swiping one of the chair legs from underneath Alex, taking him by surprise. The leg came flying off like a cricket stump being uprooted by a fast delivery. He was shaken but managed to regain his balance on the remaining three legs.

'The second pillar of life is of course money and work. I dropped out of university and became a drifter, unable to hold onto a job. If that had been you our parents would have of course supported you financially to get you back on your feet!' Again, the hammer was swung. This time Alex was more prepared. He tried to repel the tool with his mind. Lance grimaced as he battled against the invisible force that felt like a magnet keeping the hammer at bay. Alas for Alex it was no use as his older brother used his physical strength to power through Alex's relatively weak mind control, sending another wooden support cart-wheeling drunkenly across the room. Alex tottered precariously but just maintained his position on the two chair legs that remained.

Lance continued on his obviously rehearsed diatribe. 'The third of the pillars of a happy life is health. You even seemed to be able to charm the germs, or perhaps send them in my direction as I spent weeks at a time bedridden with various maladies as a child. I used to watch you enviously through the window over my bed as you frolicked gaily in the sun. I will admit you did once get chicken pox but you were over it in a matter of days and of course not before you passed it on, condemning me to three agonising weeks of a vicious circle of itching and scratching as I tried to sleep fitfully on an air-bed.' Without warning Lance pulled his arm back and swiped a third leg with the mallet. On this occasion Alex did not have time to mentally deter his brother and was sent spinning like a top. He eventually managed to keep his balance on the stool, precariously positioned as he was with just one solitary leg intact.

'And now for the last but most definitely the most important pillar…love.' Murdoch spat out this last statement, laughing with a false, ironic cackle. 'You had the pick of girls all through your adolescent years. There was always a gaggle of 'lovelies' ready to fight for the right to even be near you. And what did I get?' Murdoch whispered with a sneer as he lent in close to his sibling's face. 'I got your cast-offs and other silly bints who went out with me just in an attempt to get to you!'

Alex braced himself for the inevitable as the last leg of the stool was forcefully removed. He came crashing to the floor in a heap, his bound hands unable to control his short fall. He winced as his posterior went numb from the hard landing.

Murdoch sighed slowly as if unseating his brother so violently and dramatically had been a wonderful release of pressure. 'Still, I am willing to let bygones be bygones and now I have vented my anger I will be letting you go unharmed'.

Alex breathed a little easier but did not relax completely, unsure his long-lost brother was telling the truth, confused by the supposed change of heart.

'Yes, you will be free to rejoin your friends but not before I do a bit of…how should I phrase it…'rebalancing'. You see, I have found a way to enjoy some of the powers you gained naturally although unfortunately for you this does mean all of your powers being transferred to me!'

Murdoch bent down to grab Alex's shoulders. The stricken sibling tried to shimmy away but he was hampered by his tight bonds that still tied him to the seat of the ruined stool. Murdoch seized his brother, roughly turning him through 90 degrees to face a spinning black and white disc on the wall that Alex had not noticed before. Alex instantly became mesmerized by the swirling pattern, unable to avert his eyes as his breathing slowed.

21

At the old church in Steeple Hill there was now a congenial air as Stump and his mother were deep in conversation, catching up on years of missed birthdays and separate experiences and memories. The women from LIFT had kindly put on a brew and half a packet of 'own brand' biscuits (leftover from Sunday School the previous weekend) were being passed around. The recent revelations were all too much for Herbert though who was slunk behind the altar, popping painkillers as if they were parma violets to cure his newly developed headache.

As the congregation were engrossed in conversation, a young woman slunk past them undetected. The young woman, no other than Hannah, disappeared past them all and snuck up the spiral staircase that led to the belfry and the disintegrating church tower. Moments later there was an almighty rumbling tumult, stronger than any that had accompanied the earth tremors earlier that day that.

'The giants are here! The giants are here! Everyone save yourselves!' wailed the now mentally deranged priest who had unscrewed a bottled of communion wine and was taking large gulps, straight from the bottle.

When the rumbling abated, Stump bravely rushed outside to see what had caused the latest mighty shuddering. He soon saw that the cause was not the oversized beasts but something much closer to home. All around him gravestones lay smashed and broken under the weight of several large stones. He looked up. When he had last gazed upwards, the tall tower had pointed proudly towards the sky. But now it was protruding outwards, level with the ground but suspended several yards in the air. It was if it had been forced downwards on a giant hinge pivoted on the belfry. Now horizontal and pointing south west towards the sun and the city centre. (Bizarrely the tower had shed its stone to reveal that it was not entirely hollow inside. The spire that now pointed away from the church was in fact a gleaming metallic cone, glowing fiercely in the sun and beautifully patterned with a spiral motif.

Stump now shifted his gaze to the base of the tapering conical structure. There, where the spire met the now roofless but largely intact belfry, he spotted a fleck of red against the dark bat-friendly interior. He knew it could only be his housemate Hannah.

He rushed back inside past the startled others and began to make his way towards the steps that led up the tower, throwing back the fading red curtain but halting at the base of the spiral steps. Despite a haste to ensure his housemate was okay, he could not help but pause as he looked at the wall at the bottom of the steps. The surface was not bare stone and mortar as in most churches of this age but plastered to a smooth finish. Not only that but some sort of mural had been delicately etched into its surface, the indentations filled with dark paint. Staring at the strange depictions, at first he did not hear the footsteps echoing down the stone flags from above. He looked up to see Hannah coming down to meet him.

'Quite amazing isn't it? The mural winds its way all the way to the belfry, depicting a journey though time,' said Hannah, conveying mild excitement.

Stump did not reply as he continued to stare at the simple pictures, his advanced brain attempting to establish their meanings.

Hannah appeared to read his mind and, not waiting for him to ask, offered her insight. 'The first picture appears to be the start of the story, the two giants with Avona in the distance.' The sketch was faint, the once sharp image having faded over the centuries due to exposure to light and other natural processes but two large sticks figures could still be made out. A smaller figure with long hair stood on a ridge overlooking a desolate landscape. 'I think the next scene depicts when the giants next appeared, back in roman times,' continued Hannah, moving up a few steps as she spoke, sounding like a lecturer rather than the student she was actually assumed to be. This sketch showed many more stick men this time, possibly an army in regimented formation wearing armour and helmets as at their feet mighty catapults hurled burning missiles through the misty air. 'And lastly...' finished Hannah, '...this panel shows an encounter from around a millennia ago, if the clothing and style of housing is a good indication of the age.' The drawing showed long thatched huts arranged haphazardly and enclosed by tall fences of wooden stakes driven into the ground. People in simple garb were shown running in fear away from two giant figures.

'The giants appear around every thousand years it seems then?' mused Stump.

'Yes, the evidence does seem to show that,' Hannah replied thoughtfully.

'And in each case the giants disappeared only to return again?'

'Yes, indeed...also true.'

'Meaning nobody has been able to stop them so far!'

Hannah paused to think before answering with care. 'There is a first time for everything!' she said uncertainly with a wan smile before moving the subject on. 'There is one last frieze in the belfry which may provide the key to defeating them but I cannot make any sense of it!' Hannah gestured for Stump to follow her up the last few steps to look at the fresco, hoping that his extra brainpower could unlock the hidden meaning.

Now upstairs in the belfry, Stump probed hopefully into the corners of his tobacco pouch, eking out the very last dry remnants of his strawberry and vanilla flavoured tobacco before pressing the dry strands gently into the bowl of his pipe. In front of him Hannah was bent down, examining the last of the stone etchings she had found.

This final tile was clearly quite different from those that preceded it, being chiselled into stone rather than merely painted or drawn on the surface. This depiction was also on the belfry floor itself, rather than the previous pictures that had been painted on the walls of the stairwell leading to this point.

'I just can't make head nor tail of it', said Hannah, shaking her head.

'I would have thought you'd be more concerned with working that out!' replied Stump, pointing out into the open air where the spinning metallic core of the old spire jutted away from them.

'Oh I know what that is. That is just the weapon we use to slay the giants. That is clear enough from the pictures that adorn the staircase. What we really need to work out is the key, the legend if you will. Namely how we fire the thing up!'

'And you think it has something to do with this final etching?' said Stump, unsure he would be of any assistance.

'Yes, definitely! Look here,' she said, pointing to one side of the grid of squares that formed the last pictorial message on the floor. 'There is a shallow channel around the outside of the grid which then goes up the wall and directly into the base of the weapon.'

Stump frowned. To him it just looked like a strange grid of squares forming something not unlike a 'noughts & crosses' board. However, instead of there being an 'X' or an 'O' drawn in each box there was a hand-print, a foot-print or duck's foot carved into the stone. Within each box there was printed a single letter that was either an 's' or 'd'. Off to one side of the grid, at the top left hand corner as they looked at it, there was another circular indentation not mentioned by Hannah. The hollow was about a foot across, an inch deep and at its centre a pointer was positioned. It resembled a compass although there were no bearings printed around its edge, only letters and pictures that matched those within the 'noughts and crosses' grid next to it.

Before Hannah and Stump could muse any longer, they heard footsteps coming up the staircase behind them. They waited with apprehension, wondering who would appear from around the corner. They both smiled broadly as Alex and one of the ducks calmly walked towards them.

'Thank goodness you are alright!' shrieked Hannah, rushing towards Alex to embrace him. It was an awkward clinch as he kept his arms limply by his side, not returning Hannah's warming clinch. She stepped back and looked him up and down in surprise as if something in the way he looked would explain his new emotionless demeanour.

'You are okay aren't you?' prodded Hannah.

'Yes of course I am. I had a spot of bother but nothing I couldn't sort out by myself, he frigidly replied.

Hannah was not convinced. She detected an odd change of character in Alex but with no time to ponder further she pressed on regardless. 'Alex, we think this is some sort of weapon but we cannot figure out how to use it.'

Alex merely nodded sagely.

'However, we have a second problem. We need the giants in the right position in front of the weapon before we can fire it.'

Alex squinted as he looked out to the bright exterior, shielding his eyes from the glare.

'I need to ask you to bring the giants to us,' continued Hannah. 'I know I am asking a lot but it's the only way we can defeat them. Can you use your car to do that? Perhaps they could follow you and you can drive fast enough to keep them at a safe distance.' Hannah's expression was pained, unsure how Alex would respond to the dangerous request.

Alex paused before responding. 'I'll do my best', he said quietly before robotically walking off.

22

Alex walked out of the ruined church and looked at his car that was parked outside the house, only a few yards away. He raised his arm to call his pride and joy over towards him. His recent companion, the illusionist duck, stood to one side, cocking his neck to look up at him.

'Its not working,' he said more to himself than the duck, as he turned his hand over and over as if the explanation would appear in the patterns of palm-lines. 'Its no use, I have lost all my powers!'

'Well, you don't need your powers to drive do you? Just walk over and lets get in the thing,' said the magical duck, unsympathetically.

Alex had known something was wrong as soon as he had rejoined the others in the church, not that he could put his finger on what the issue was. As he thought more deeply he realised he could not remember walking to the church or what he had done in the last hour. Whatever it was had resulted in his powers being removed just as he had been getting used to wielding his newly untapped mental strength.

He solemnly walked over to his car but perked up a little as he opened the doors remotely with a soft 'plip' of his key fob, anticipating the drive ahead. At least he knew his power as a good driver was almost certainly still in force. 'Brace yourself duck, for the drive of your life. But first, it's a beautiful day so lets have the roof down.' The nervous duck had already buckled himself in. He had already seen what the car could do without a driver, let alone with its crazed owner in the driving seat.

'So…' the duck said apprehensively. 'How are we going to get the giants towards the church? What are we going to do?'

Alex looked over at the duck with eyebrows raised. 'The question isn't what *are* we going to do, the question is what *aren't* we going to do!' And with that Alex donned his expensive shades, turned the key in the ignition and the car burst into life with a triumphant roar. The duck was pressed back into the passenger seat as they sped away with venomous acceleration, leaving a snaking double trail of rubber in their wake.

They drifted and swerved around the sharp and narrow walled corners of the ancient thoroughfare before reaching the crest of Bell Hill where at great pace the car literally took off. It glided through the air in a graceful arc but was forced to meet the ground once again half way down the slope with a squeak of pain from the slick tyres.

It turned out the giants were not difficult to track. With the roof down Alex could hear the sound of their mighty growls, even above the melodious rhythm of his engine. They hurtled through the old neighbourhoods of Bristol, once separate proud villages that now formed one urban mass, Alex enjoying the new chicanes in the road created by hastily abandoned vehicles, scattered as if cast like seeds by an almighty hand.

The duo of man and duck pressed on, the car groaning up the steep incline of Park Street before tearing along Whiteladies Road, finally screeching to a halt at the great open park known locally as The Downs. At times Alex's 'enthusiastic' driving style had threatened to eject his feathered companion but the seat belt meant the bird luckily just managed to stay within the interior of the open-topped car. This was fortunate indeed as now outside the car, barely a few yards away, the two giants stalked.

The beasts had yet to spot the pair as the car was partially shielded by some tall trees. The warring brothers were also unlikely to notice anyone or anything else as they were too engrossed in uprooting the tall pines that sparsely bordered the grassy plain, hurling them effortlessly at each other as they sparred. It would surely only be a matter of time though before the gesturing stopped and they physically clashed, not caring what or who would be crushed beneath them in their wake.

Alex plucked up the courage to slowly edge his car out from behind the screening of the trees. Out in the open he expected the giants to spot him immediately so he kept the powerful engine purring with his foot hovering above the accelerator pedal, ready to pull away in an instant with the giants in tow.

Alex waited and waited but the giants failed to notice him. He looked over to the duck in the vain hope of inspiration.

'You know what we need?' said the duck.

'No, but I am sure you are going to tell me!'

'They are too preoccupied with each other to bother with little you and me, despite their indiscriminate hatred,' the duck stated plainly. 'We need to be more conspicuous. What we need is a bigger car.'

Alex looked a little crestfallen. 'Well, wouldn't we all. I would love a Ferrari, Lamborghini or a Bugatti but I just don't have that much money!'

'I didn't mean a slightly bigger car, I meant a *much* bigger car!'

Alex placed his left arm over the headrest to turn to the duck and give him his full attention. 'And how exactly do you propose we get a *much* bigger car?'

'A simple matter of illusion my dear boy. All I need is a small mirror and a large sheet.'

'I do have a sheet in the boot I use for picnics of course but I don't think I can help with the mirror.'

'Oh I think you can,' said the duck.

Instinctively Alex moved his hands to protect his expensive, designer rear-view mirror.

'Do you want to get rid of the giants or not?' asked the duck, condescendingly. 'Besides, there is a fairly good chance you'll get it back in one piece'. After a moments hesitation, Alex reluctantly detached the mirror, as painfully as if he was pulling out one of his own fingernails.

Clutching the expensive piece of glass, the duck half leapt, half flew out of the passenger seat with a flutter. He opened the boot and removed the large gingham sheet with a flourish and a swish, wielding the large piece of material with ease, despite his small size. The duck threw the sheet neatly over the vehicle as Alex leapt clear, just before it completely engulfed his car.

The duck stalked slowly and steadily, waving his arms with an element of drama, looking left and right as he wafted his wings as if playing to an invisible crowd. Alex looked on jealously, wishing he still had the powers to aid his diminutive cohort and ultimately his housemates. The duck turned to the car making upward motions with his wings. Gradually the sheet rose until it bellowed out like a sail, the car still hidden behind its great expanse. Then with another flamboyant gesture the duck brought his wings down again swiftly, like a conductor signalling the triumphant end to an orchestral performance. Without being touched the sheet fell away and Alex's car was revealed once more, although it was nearly four times its original size!

Alex gawped in awe. It was his car only so much bigger. What could have been better! He ran to his beauty but stopped as he got nearby, desperately wondering how he was going to reach the door handle that was now well above his head. Just as he was about to haul himself up onto a tyre that was nearly at head height, the duck put a wing in front of his legs to gently stop him in his tracks.

'Remember, it's an illusion' urged the bird. 'Open the door as you normally would.' Disbelieving but with no time to distrust, Alex closed his eyes and reached forward, feeling for where the handle would be if his old car had been in the same position. To his immense surprise he felt the familiar cold metal in his hand and the satisfying click as the door opened when he pulled. Without looking he lowered himself into the driving seat, half expecting to fall back down to earth with a bump but instead his posterior met the cushioned upholstery. Opening his eyes once more he looked around to see the inside of the car. Everything was comfortingly a normal size.

It really was an illusion as the duck had said, as simple as that. Curiosity got the better of Alex and he opened the door again slightly to peer out the side. It looked as though the door had opened in the middle of one of the giant wheels. Above him the car stretched up to the open roof. Feeling disorientated and more than a little sick, he decided it was best to close the door and not do that again.

'How on earth did you do this with just a sheet and a mirror, duck? a perplexed Alex enquired.

'A true magician never reveals his secrets Alex,' replied the duck. 'All I can say is that objects in the rear view mirror may appear larger than they are.'

If the giants noticed the new larger vehicle in their midst they deemed it as neither a threat nor a nuisance as they continued to ignore it. Alex changed their outlook by racing towards the giants who were now sparring 'toe to toe'. The skilful driver advanced onto the right foot of the first giant, bumping the car deliberately into its little toe. The giant reeled in pain but before the colossus could react Alex reversed, turned the steering wheel and sped on again, intercepting the other oversized being, crashing into the soft under parts of its left sole. The huge brothers now both cried in pain and looked down at what annoyance had caused their discomfort. Spotting the whirling metal creature in the grass they both moved to pounce and quash the small irritant.

Seeing the giants finally pursuing them as planned, Alex made haste. The duck sat beside him again in the passenger seat, clearly concentrating hard to maintain the illusion of the over-sized car. Alex hoped that nothing would distract the feathered magician.

The car moved away and increased in speed, skidding on the parkland and showering the bare feet of the great creatures with freshly mown grass and mud. Despite the evident danger Alex was relaxed as he was sure he could outpace his pursuers. In truth he envisaged the only difficulty would be ensuring that the giants stayed within the sights of the weapon at the church long enough to be fired upon. Of course that assumed that the others had now figured out how to work the mysterious contraption. If not, then all his efforts would be in vain. Again he regretted not having his powers, thinking how much easier this would be with his other-worldly means of persuasion.

Alex raced down into the centre of the city, seeing the giants close behind him when he dared to look over his shoulder. Everything was going to plan so far and the driver relaxed a little more.

Before long they neared the village of Steeple Hill and could just make out the eerie glow of the spire high on the hillside.

A look to his left reassured Alex that the duck was still in mental control, maintaining the illusion of the giant sports car. The strain of sustaining the parlour trick was clearly starting to show on the bird though as beads of sweat were forming, flattening the feathers around its head.

Before Alex could ponder on whether he had ever seen a duck sweat before, the expression of the duck's face unexpectedly changed as it lifted his head to sniff the air feverishly. Alex looked ahead and could immediately see what had broken the meditation of the fowl. A few yards up the road he could see a large bakery. In the chaos and looting that had followed the arrival of the giants, the door had been left wide open. Bread of all shapes and sizes was strewn all over the pavement outside, many loaves even spilling into the road. With the roof of the convertible down, the odour was clearly irresistible to the duck's sensitive sense of smell.

Alex pre-empted what was going to happen next. He locked the doors and lunged for the dashboard, pressing the button that closed the roof but the mechanism did not respond. He then realised with horror he was going too fast to close the roof and he knew if he slowed down to trap the duck it would be suicide as the giants would catch up with them in seconds.

Unable to resist the delicious odour any longer, the duck took flight out of the car. Alex tried to grab the bird as it fluttered past but all he clasped were a couple of mangy tail feathers. He poked his head above the windscreen to see what the car looked like to the outside world. As he feared, with the duck gone the powers of illusion had also departed and his car would look small and insignificant once more to the giants. He had no time to stop and grab the duck, who was now outside the bakery, happily pecking into a stale sun-dried tomato loaf after first nibbling at a ciabatta.

Alex knew he had to find another way to grab the attention of the giants and fast as he could see they were already losing interest in him. They had stopped their pursuit, now preferring to pick off chimneys from the houses along the road and hurling the dusty brick structures at each other.

Taking action, the young driver sped back towards the towering beasts at great speed, revving the engine at every opportunity and drifting round corners as if the surface underneath him was made of ice and not tarmac. These exact sort of manoeuvres never failed to attract attention and this was time was no exception. (Although, judging by the snarls on the face of the giants, their reaction was equally negative when compared to previous viewers of these type of 'antics'.) At least the ploy had worked as the giants threw down their chimneys and concentrated on pursuing Alex, the little irritant, once again.

Alex pulled away quickly with the giants in tow once more, white smoke filling the air from his expensive tyres. In the hastily replaced rear view mirror he could see the giants swishing their meaty hands, attempting to swat him and the car he drove but he smiled, now enjoying the game he was playing with these dumb creatures.

He looked towards the church and the weapon that pulsed ominously as they sped ever closer. Nearly home, Alex powered up the final hill towards the others. The giants were now slowing their pace as they transferred their gaze from the car at their feet to the glowing spire ahead of them, forgetting about Alex.

It was when there was less than two hundred yards for Alex to drive that he realised with some horror there was something wrong. He was pumping the accelerator but nothing was happening. The roaring engine had abruptly stopped dead. Still rolling up the hill (but with ever diminishing momentum) he turned the key to try and kick his little devil back into life but nothing stirred apart from a sad repetitive whining, all the dials on the dashboard gliding sadly towards their resting places.

Admitting defeat, Alex applied the handbrake before gravity had a chance to express its force that would result in an inevitable slide back down the slope towards the rapidly approaching giants. He knew he could not stay stationary for long as he was now in mortal danger of being crushed by an advancing giant's foot but even contemplating that grisly fate he was reluctant to leave his beautiful car behind. Frozen in a quandary he could only stare back at the giants (or more accurately at their giant feet) as they were planted ominously close to his small, fragile frame.

Finally Alex stirred himself into action and decided to try and save what he could from his car before making good his escape. However, in reaching for his cashmere scarf that was laying neatly on the parcel shelf the sweater he was wearing became entangled with the handbrake. He tried to wrench himself free but every movement only resulted in him being more entwined. With one final yank he gained his release at some cost.

Alex frowned as he examined the hole that he had created in his costly pullover. Still, this was soon to be the least of his worries as in his struggles Alex had not only accidentally released the handbrake but pulled it clear from its housing. As he rather vocally and colourfully bemoaned the surprisingly shoddy German engineering standards on that part of his beloved, the rest of the car was now rolling back down the hill and gaining speed with each revolution of the well-polished wheels with Alex still inside dimly clutching the detached phallus. With no way to stop the runaway he considered jumping out of the open roof but that would certainly cause injury (or at the very least a nasty graze and some letting of blood, a liquid notoriously difficult to remove from delicate fabrics.)

With the engine inactive, the brakes would have no effect and so with resigned dismay he knew the only way to stop the vehicle was by deliberately crashing it. Unfortunately the only suitable object on a downhill trajectory was the exposed big toe of the nearest giant, a happenstance that was not very appealing. Alex braced himself, closed his eyes and feared for the worst.

He was surprised as he waited for an impact that never came. Sadly this was by no means a blessing as he felt himself being lifted from the car by its open roof.

He kept his eyes firmly shut, not wanting to witness at first hand the horrors that were about to befall him. Accepting his fate, he did not squirm at the hands of the giant as he swung through the air, the only sound he could hear being the urgent flapping of wings.

Hold on a minute, he thought. The urgent flapping of wings? With a dollop of apprehension Alex opened his eyes and looked up. Instead of seeing an oversized hand wrapped around his shirt collar he saw the duck who had abandoned him earlier for a stale loaf of bread, its beak tightly gripping the lapel of his shirt. Now far below, Alex winced as he heard the crunching and twisting of metal as his beautiful car was undoubtedly being mangled under the bare feet of the giants. He kept his gaze skywards, not willing to witness such painful and mindless destruction.

He wanted to ask the duck why it had returned but thought it best to wait until he was safely back on the ground as if he duck moved its beak to speak it would more than likely have to release its tenuous hold.

Shortly, the duck and the boy came into land gracefully at the foot of the church. Alex shook himself down as the duck ruffled its feathers from head to toe. Alex knew he should have been angry with the duck for leaving him in peril but that emotion had been replaced with relief at being saved once more. 'Thanks for coming back for me,' he said unsurely, still not used to conversing with talking birds.

'That's alright', replied the duck. 'The bread was a little dry anyway.' Alex scowled a little at the unrepentant duck but there was no time for recriminations as they both raced through the echoing body of the church and up the spiral staircase to join the housemates.

23

The incongruous group of ducks and humans stood together in the battered belfry, secretly each hoping the other would somehow hold the answer to the puzzle that was etched out before them in ancient stone. Despite being collectively devoid of ideas, everyone was keen for some sort of action, especially Alex it seemed as he was the one to break the uncomfortable silence.

'Um, I realise we are all striving to find a solution to save the world here', said Alex uncertainly. 'But if we can't do that, can we at least save ourselves?' he proposed with a cheesy grin as he quietly stepped backwards a pace or two, towards the spiral steps. 'After all, it appears that now we have gained the attention of those two beasts we don't quite know what to do with them!' finished the prim student, pointing out of the gaping hole and on towards the captivated gargantuans.

Everyone stopped looking at the floor, turning their uncertain gaze to where Alex's manicured finger was pointing. The ducks even extended their longs necks to take in the view. The two giants were mesmerized by the spinning, shining, golden conical structure aimed at their mighty girths but how long would the huge creatures be transfixed by the weapon and would they be able to fire it in time?

Hannah at last regained her composure. 'Right, we need to focus. There must be an answer here somewhere in this damn pattern.' She scanned the hieroglyphs like a grandmaster at chess trying to calculate their options against the pressure of a ticking clock. The 'clever' duck weaved between her legs and stopped with his left foot placed neatly inside one of the duck feet shaped indentations.

'This is no time for fooling around, duck', said Hannah, roughly pushing the small creature out of the way.

'Au contraire' the duck replied, 'I think I have worked it out. It's a game! The one that ties you up in knots. Quick, I need the rest of you to join in!'

'WHAT?!' The rest of the group replied in a staggered un-sonorous chorus.

'Why surely its obvious!', the duck continued unabashed, 'Its merely an ancient game of Twister!'

'Right, that's it. You are going on the barbeque,' threatened Alex, producing a recently sharpened knife from his boot-strap. The duck instinctively flinched and fluttered away. Outside the giants were looming nearer on the horizon. Slowly but very surely they were approaching with menace, still transfixed by the spire but a look of wanton destruction beginning to return in their huge eyes.

'No wait!' shouted Hannah, grabbing the lethal sabre from Alex just in time. 'The daft duck may just be on to something.' Hannah stalked over to the strange circular dial on the floor to peer at it again in more detail. She gently took hold of one end of the pointer and span it with some force. It whirred around for a few revolutions, scraping the polished stone underneath it, sounding like two small millstones grinding corn. Everyone looked on silently, many pairs of eyes revolving in their sockets in time with the mechanism until after a few seconds it came to rest on a picture of a human hand in a square with the letter 's' neatly scored with a flourish.

'Well, if this really is like Twister, it must be one of us humans who needs to put their hand there,' said Stump helpfully, pointing to a picture of a human hand next to the letter 's' as he puffed thoughtfully on his pipe.

'But whose hand?' Hannah replied. 'None of our names begin with 's', or 'd' for that matter.'

'What about 'sirs' and 'dames'?' proffered Alex, 'A bit old fashioned but this may date from the middle ages after all.'

'Worth a shot!' replied Hannah, 'Please, after you!'

Despite a slight reluctance to take the plunge, the sight of the giants marauding ever nearer ensured Alex bravely stepped forward. He stood with feet together at the base of the ancient markings as if preparing to leap into choppy waters of an unknown depth before he steadfastly placed his right foot, onto the indicated square, trying to ignore the obvious comparisons to a certain adventure film from the 80's.

For a moment nothing happened. Alex looked around the room expectantly, as if someone would have an explanation as to why this move had not worked. But then suddenly the now horizontal spire outside dimmed as the floor beneath Alex's foot glowed red hot. He removed his foot and screamed in pain as the searing heat rose through the leather of his high-priced hand-made shoe and onto his bare foot. He hoped off, clutching his scorched tootsies as the spire outside regained its eerie illumination.

'That obviously wasn't the right way to play the game,' Hannah mused, stroking her chin.

'You surprise me!' said Alex with no subtle sarcasm as he crouched on the floor, blowing on his glowing foot to assuage the burning sensation. 'Wasn't this clever duck meant to have all the answers anyway?' he said with an angry accusatory shimmy of his head towards the bird in question.

'Simply not the case I'm afraid. Sometimes, I have to leave you stupid humans to your own devices. I am just here to guide you in the right direction. I never said I had all the answers,' the duck retorted, with more pomposity than the occasion warranted.

'What did you say?' demanded Hannah, shaking the duck fiercely.

'I said, 'I never said I had all the answers.''

'No, no. Before that.'

'I left you to your own devices? I'm here to guide you in the right direction?' said the duck unsurely.

'That could be it!' Hannah unceremoniously moved the duck out of the way and turned back to the stencilled game in front of her. Everyone held their breaths as Hannah placed her left foot where Alex had placed his right peg only a moment before. Everyone braced themselves but this time nothing happened. Hannah allowed herself a smile but no one else did as they did not grasp the breakthrough the academic had made.

'Quick! Someone spin the wheel again,' she said, waving her arm in encouragement without taking her eyes from the floor.

Gingerly Stump took the pipe out of his mouth and stepped over to the wheel. Forgetting his strength he gave the indicator an almighty swish. After making a sound like a devilish mortar and pestle for a good few seconds, the stone needle came to rest. 'I have a picture of a duck and the letter 'd' said Stump in his clear Yorkshire accent.

'Right. One of the ducks. Place your right flapper in the corresponding square,' instructed Hannah. The magic duck slowly waddled over and dutifully placed his webbed member in the shallow hollow. Again nothing happened.

'I think we've got it! It was the duck who unwittingly cracked half the problem in what he said a minute ago. When he talked about us being 'left to our own devices' and going in the 'right direction' I knew we had to use our left and right hands and feet to cover the squares, like a true game of Twister. At first I could not work out what the 's' and 'd' referred to though. But then I remembered what you said Alex. You were correct that the game was etched in the middle ages but the language used in a church at that time would not have been English, it would have been Latin'!

'Therefore 'sinistro' for 'left' and 'dextro' for right,' concluded the quiz buff Stump.

'Exactly. Someone spin it again!' The dial was duly rapidly rotated again and again, so that an increasingly complex tangle of avian and human appendances began to fill the squares. Each player became more contorted and uncomfortable as arms and legs became ever more entwined when each new instruction was called out. Nobody dared (or were able to) look outside as the giants made progress to where they all stood precariously in a variety of over-stretched poses.

After only a couple of minutes of play, all of the players, man, woman and duck alike, were struggling to maintain their balance. This was not helped when one of the ducks sneezed as Hannah's long and ticklish locks were draped too close to its beak. Hannah herself found her nose uncomfortably near to Stump's posterior and Alex was now embarrassingly close to Hannah's décolletage.

Just at the point when Alex felt himself tipping into Hannah's bosom, the last square in the grid was finally filled by a left hand of unknown origin. Then something mysterious started to happen. An orange viscous liquid welled up between the squares in sticky globules, eventually joining until the whole grid was bordered by the brightly coloured fluid.

One of the ducks sneezed again, causing Hannah to lose poise as she understandably turned away from the spray of mucous droplets. She careered into Stump and men, women and ducks all came tumbling down like an un-shapely set of colourful dominos.

Everyone pulled further away as the rivulets broke their banks, swamping each square until the whole area glowed and pulsed. The fluid then flowed down from the grid, following the channels towards the outer wall before it defied gravity like tree sap by climbing the few inches to the base of the great weapon that was now spinning with increased fury. The liquid then slunk along down the spiral channel etched into the side of the weapon like magnetic engine oil until the whole spire was coated in the strange substance. This all occurred not a moment too soon as the giants were now almost at the end of the ancient graveyard that encircled the church.

The weapon pulsed faster and faster, the sound waves it created resonating against the stone walls as the volume built, forcing the occupants to cover their ears in a hopeless attempt to block out the terrible low frequency buzz.

The giants were now barely a few feet away, their faces and limbs contorted in a maelstrom of emotions as they jostled to be the first to reach the incandescent weapon, both mesmerised like wasps following the overpowering scent of sweet spilt beer.

The first to reach the spire was Vincent. Tentatively he lowered his hand to just behind the spinning point before touching it lightly. The giant clearly felt little adverse response as he then grasped the spinning weapon, smiling ominously at the group in the half-destroyed belfry.

'He's trying to slow the weapon down!' Hannah shouted above the din.

'I wouldn't say he was trying,' replied Alex, 'I would say that he is succeeding!' They all now agreed as the revolutions slowed before their eyes. Vincent's hands were now tightly clasped around the spire, gripping it tighter and tighter until it almost stopped turning completely. The weapon appeared to be losing its power as the eerie orange light from the liquid that enveloped it noticeably dulled.

'I don't understand why it isn't working?' fretted Hannah. 'What else do we need to do?'

'No idea,' scoffed Stump. 'But if this is going to be our last moments on this earthly plane, I would prefer a full cup of tea!' The tweed-wearer thrust his half-empty cup forward with gallows humour to emphasise the point. A drip of the dark liquid fell to the floor and into one of the dimming rivulets of orange that fed the fading spire. Somehow the tea was a shot in the arm for the strange contraption, sending a pulse of brighter light to the end of the weapon. For a moment Vincent removed his hands as if he had received a small electric shock but within seconds he had replaced them on the device as it began to dim and slow once more.

'Are you sure you are just drinking tea? Hannah asked quickly.

'Well, I do like a special blend, it is very strong and powerful,' replied a surprised Stump.

'Whatever it is, it seems to be helping,' said Alex as he wrenched the mug out of Stump's hand and poured the entire contents on the floor, much to the Yorkshire-man's utter dismay.

The tea spread through the grid of channels at their feet, mixing and bubbling angrily like boiling magma. The substance coursed through the device and along the weapon. Without warning the mechanism discharged, emitting its deadly orange ray and wiping the smile from Vincent's face and that of his brother behind him. Vincent was struck squarely in the chest by the ray, his deep cries reverberating as he was thrown backwards and upwards by the immense fury of the machine.

The group in the tower watched as his lifeless body was propelled out of sight, many miles to the south and west. His brother Goram could only watch on in horror, not possessing the time or guile to avoid the same fate as the weapon fired again and he too was hurled far and away on a similar trajectory.

The weapon spent, the glow and its orange life-force drained through a small aperture in the base of the outer wall before the entire contraption crashed to the soft ground beneath. Silence followed that was soon shattered as everyone began to celebrate the demise of the giants who had ruined a perfectly good day of scholarly avoidance. Everyone celebrated that was apart from Hannah who remained quiet and still, staring out in the direction of where the beasts had been flung.

'Cheer up old misery guts,' said Stump, rather firmly slapping the flaxen-haired lass on the back. 'Those giants are dead and gone. Deceased. Evaporated. Expunged. Or whatever other more eloquent adjective you may wish to use from your Oxbridge days.'

'I wish I could share your confidence,' replied Hannah. 'I just need to be sure.' Gradually the others sensed Hannah's air of malcontent and their revelry was more than an iota becalmed. When she ushered one of the ducks over to her, they became even more restless. The duck responded to her signalling by stepping forward with a feathery salute.

'I need you for a scouting mission,' she said as she stooped down with her hands on her knees to address the small creature as one would speak to a small child.

Without the need for another word, the duck clearly knew what was expected. It ungainly waddled up to the gaping hole in the belfry and stepped over the parapet, dropping a few feet before finding its wings and slowly flapping its way into the distance towards the south and west. The duck flew noisily, every downward stroke of its short wingspan accompanied with a soft quack.

It looked ahead as it flew but rarely below. If it had looked down it would have had a great view of the devastation wrecked by the giants. Great swathes of the city were affected along the paths the careless beasts had earlier trod, their tracks resembling the devastation normally caused by a pair of twisting tornados. Only a few houses were lucky and had remained intact, their proud roofs jutting skywards amongst the smoking rubble and grey dust.

On through the city centre the duck flew, using thermals to gain height, the once busy streets below now solemn and deserted. Finally the duck spied the glistening waters of the River Avon.

Tired after a long flight for a small duck, the bird sought a resting place and was rewarded by an ornate bridge that over-looked the sluggish waters. After a quick preen it extended its neck and casually looked below. There it saw the waters flowing around two huge bodies that caused the river to eddy and swirl behind them. It could see that both figures were lying on their backs and they were very large as the deep tidal water only reached half way up the sides of their bodies. Their chests were scarred and blackened, encircled by a deep scarlet ring.

The eyesight of a duck is excellent so after only a few seconds it was convinced that even from quite a distance it could spy movement from the giants down below. However, it was sure that the creatures were not stirring and it was merely the force of the water being occasionally sufficient to nudge the arms of the dead bodies a few inches one way or another. Satisfied there was no danger present here, the duck began to make a slow turn and readied itself to take flight, returning with the good news.

The duck pushed its feet into the top of the wall that fringed the bridge, propelling its little body into the air. Taking one last look at the carcasses in the water it flapped its wings to gain height but just as it turned a movement registered in the corner of one eye. Deciding it was better to be safe than sorry, the duck performed a wide u-turn and swooped down for a closer look, gliding down to the muddy river edge and landing with a wet plop.

With a level of caution finely honed from eons of its kind being nearer the bottom of the food chain, the duck waddled over to the nearest giant and looked at its pale face. It soon concluded there was no sign of life. The mouth was gaping half open and water swilled in and out of the opening like a sea-cave at high tide and the eyelids were firmly shut. The only movement was an arm, moving gently

143

back and forth with the eddies as if it were waving to invisible passers-by. But then without warning the giant's hand extended at lightening pace, grabbing hold of one of the duck's legs. The startled bird managed to shake itself free after a short struggle and a loud squawk, flying off at great pace back towards Steeple Hill, now the bearer of bad tidings.

Hannah did not have to wait for a verbal response from the duck on its return. The wild eyes and hurried crash-landing spoke a thousand words. With sadness and growing apprehension she realised they had failed.

24

'This isn't over I'm afraid people,' Hannah said. 'We need to get over to the gorge as quickly as possible. The giants are still alive.'

A collective slump spread through the camp before Stump spoke for them all.

'And how exactly do you suppose we do that?' he replied with his usual healthy scepticism. 'Walking would take us over an hour, the only car at our disposal has been crushed and its not as though there is any public transport running at the moment. Maybe all the ducks could link arms and form a plane which we could hop on the back of!' he said sarcastically.

Hannah pursed her lips in thought at his fanciful suggestion.

'My God, you are actually thinking about it, aren't you?!' said Stump.

'Why not? We all know these are no ordinary ducks,' Hannah stated as she made her way back down the stairs from the belfry, ushering the others to follow. They did so meekly, driven by fear, knowing that Hannah was the only person who seemed to have any idea how to combat the giants, even if the chance of success seemed to be shrinking by the minute, especially as the weapon that was built to defeat the giants had failed.

Alex was the last to leave the belfry. He looked out of the gaping hole in the wall with a long face, half expecting to see the scorched giants coming back towards him. Before he left he saw a small stone at the edge of the open belfry. Testing his powers he tried to move it even an inch with his mind but the small piece of rubble stayed resolutely in place. Annoyed, he kicked it over the edge and towards the graveyard below. He turned and followed the others down the ancient staircase, unable to see that the stone never quite met the ground but hovered a few inches above the green turf.

Now outside the church, Hannah whispered into the hidden ear of one of the ducks before thrusting it back up the tunnel Stump had emerged from some time before. After a couple of minutes, the faint rhythmic sound of marching could be heard coming back down the tunnel. Presently a solitary duck came through the opening, walked across the churchyard and stood obediently at the outside corner of the church. That duck was followed by another and another. In fact the ducks began to stream out of the tunnel in a long regimented string, like an army of ants emerging from their underground realm. The ducks formed neat lines against the crumbling walls with fifty birds in each row until the rows were some twenty deep. Hannah wasted little time in instructing the small avian wonders, telling them exactly what she wanted them to do. The others stood back and let her get on with it, their emotions ranging from despair to disbelief.

Before anyone could almost blink, the ducks rapidly set about their task of forming an implausible plane that was comprised roughly as follows - The largest ducks formed the two front wheels whereas the lightest ones were used for the long tail that lifted clear of the ground, their smaller bodies used to help with buoyancy and lift. The most powerful flyers were obviously integrated into the wings and the remainder of the thousand strong avian army made up the body of the plane.

Within minutes the duck plane was complete – a living, breathing (and unfortunately defecating) marvel of engineering and intelligence that resembled a World War I style bi-plane. Indeed it was a sight to behold, being accurate in almost every detail. Why the ducks chose to form such an old model could not be easily ascertained but perhaps it was the most comfortable and light-weight for its constituent parts even if the overall look was more than a little peculiar. From a distance it resembled an old plane that had flown through a muddy hedge, collecting leaves and dirt along the way. The normal hard lines of the plane 'shape' were softened by the bodies of the ducks and the camouflage colouring was produced by the alternating livery of brown, green and occasionally iridescent purple hues of the feathers. It was only at closer quarters that the true nature of the aircraft could be clearly seen to be what it truly was – an intricate three-dimensional mesh of live wildfowl.

Hannah was the first to step aboard and with caution she eased herself into the rear cockpit, wincing as she lowered herself onto an admittedly comfortable living seat of feathers. Her weight made a slight indentation but it was hardly noticeable, her mass spread more or less evenly amongst the hundreds of ducks beneath her. It was rather like sitting on a lovely eider down pillow she thought, except that in this case the stuffing had not been cruelly removed from its host, the feathers being still very much attached to the bodies that owned them. Although she had to admit she had never sat on a downy pillow before that had webbed feet poking out at odd angles and especially not pairs of eyes that that occasionally blinked at her.

Dutifully the others followed her onto the strange aircraft, Alex sitting behind Hannah, with Stump in the front cockpit trying to look the part as he lit up his pipe waiting to enjoy the ride. 'Tally ho and chocks away,' he shouted. If he expected movement to follow that instruction he was sadly disappointed as the duck plane remained rooted to the spot. 'What's wrong?' he asked.

Hannah turned round in her seat to face him.

'My experience of these types of aircraft is rather limited,' said Hannah, 'But doesn't someone need to start the propeller?'

Alex silently obliged, stepping out of the rear cockpit and ducking under the left wing as he made his way around to the front of the plane to make a cursory examination of the propeller. It showed itself to be made of two lines of fives ducks, holding onto each other by entwining their legs and meeting in the middle where a larger duck formed the central cone. This central duck even had plumage that resembled the spiral pattern favoured by some of the older planes. This attention to detail was lost on Alex however as he pulled on the end of one arm of the propeller with as much force as he could muster.

A real plane of the time would have uttered a lazy chugging sound in response to its propeller being tugged but this aircraft responded with a chorus of high-pitched 'quacks'. The propeller span reluctantly a couple of times before silently coming to rest once more. Alex sighed, again mourning the loss of his unearthly powers. Trying one more time, he heaved on the propeller with all his strength and thankfully the blades kicked into life. The wheels on the plane began to turn slowly and Alex hopped back in the cockpit just as the plane reached a jogging pace.

The plane then manoeuvred itself out of the churchyard and onto the road at Bell Hill, the aircraft now able to pick up some speed on the relatively wide expanse of the traffic-free road.

As the plane gained in speed, the ride for its passengers became increasingly bumpy as the ducks in the wheels took their turn to meet the tarmac below, only the brevity of their contact with the hard surface preventing injury. The occupants were surprised and a little alarmed at how quickly the aircraft accelerated, finally taking to the air in an unsettling and undulating fashion just over the crest of the hill. The breeze now created in flight was a godsend to all as it rid the cockpit of the cumulating odour that was beginning to resemble an aviary that had not been cleaned for some time.

Over the hills and thoroughfares they soared, following the path of the scout duck that had discovered the unceremonious landing place of the giants. Deep within the plane, that brave recognisance duck now acted as a rudder, guiding the whole living contraption noiselessly with its deliberately angled wingtips.

After some initial turbulence the ride was proving to be a smooth one and the humans on board actually began to enjoy themselves and let their thoughts wander. Stump enjoyed puffing on his pipe although the stiff breeze meant his tobacco was burning quicker than he would have liked and the smoke was blowing backwards into the faces of his human companions at the rear.

The mood darkened though as they neared the point where the giants lay. Frowns replaced smiles and muscles tightened as they made their decent towards the bridge. The air of gallows humour was replaced by the fear of the unwilling soldier, driven on only by a sense of duty and what might be lost to themselves and those around them if they ran in the opposite direction. Even Hannah, who always tried to give the assurance she had a cunning plan (whether she actually did or not) was biting her nails in obvious apprehension. Everyone gripped the feathery sides of the plane as it glided towards the ground, partly to brace themselves against the force of gravity but equally from fear.

The duck plane swooped lower, the glistening river Avon widening from a thin blue line to a thick cobalt snake as they prepared to land. The plane began to make its final decent, the ducks at the rear of the wings sticking out their limbs as those on the underbelly stuck out their feet, all to provide drag to slow their flight for touchdown.

A thousand eyes suddenly became transfixed however on what they saw below them. Their gaze was not directed towards the giants who were slowly and groggily getting to their feet in the sticky mud of the river, nor the glorious bridge its maker never saw finished. Every eye-line was in fact trained on a small figure dressed all in white on the cliffs above the gorge. A figure dwarfed by a huge spinning black and white disc, almost three times the height of a man and propped up on an angle using a giant A-frame.

The hypnotic circle began to exert its affects as all of the humans and most of the ducks succumbed to its mesmeric powers. At first the hypnotic effect did not appear costly as the plane continued to drift gently downwards as nearly every creature drifted off to sleep. But then the plane started to lose integrity, the sleeping ducks no longer able to grip their counterparts, their muscles slackening as they slumbered. Clumps of the plane came away from the whole, following their own trajectory as wind and gravity affected each part in a slightly different manner. A few ducks remained unaffected and they continued to flap, quack and even bite their sleeping neighbours as they attempted to maintain the cohesion of the plane with escalating desperation.

Within seconds though the handful of non-slumbering ducks had to admit defeat and took flight to at least save themselves, landing safely on the grassy cliff-tops. Their sleeping friends took a more direct route to the ground landing with a series of dull thuds. The scene was reminiscent of the opening day of game shooting season until the humans also fell, their heavier masses causing larger dents in the yielding earth.

25

Murdoch smirked as he flicked off the switch at the back of his spinning disk, the spiral circle gradually slowing to a stop as the latent energy from the now dormant motor discharged through the apparatus. The smartly dressed tyrant, still donning his striking white suit, now turned his malevolent attentions to an area a few short yards away where the scene resembled the day after a battle. Here bodies were strewn everywhere, the limbs twisted at all angles but what made this scene different to most after a skirmish was that the bodies were almost exclusively those of ducks, apart from the three larger forms that randomly appeared in their midst.

At first all that Murdoch could hear was the light breeze passing through the tall grass and the hurried sloshing of the river below. But gradually there were stirrings on the field. These slight movements were followed by audible protestations from man and foul alike. Luck had been on all their side though – every creature had escaped serious injury due to the low speed of their fall, the proximity to the ground and its spongy composition after days of heavy rain. This did nothing to aid the confusion of the students though, who were puzzled as one when they found their feet.

'What in the name of holy tea leaves happened then? Were we all knocked out in the crash?' said Stump, scrabbling around in search of his pipe, his memory of the last few minutes wiped from his memory.

'I don't know but I have a strange feeling that he might have something to do with it,' said Hannah, pointing behind the Yorkshire lad towards the squat figure of Murdoch who was confidently striding in their direction.

'Who is he? I feel like I should know him but I just cannot place the fellow,' said Alex with only the vaguest feeling of concern as he continued to brush dirt off his expensive clothes for what felt like the umpteenth time that day.

Now standing directly in front of them, Murdoch laughed before he spoke with an ugly, high pitched guffaw. 'You all know me,' he said. 'Although one of you knows me a lot better than the rest of you.'

Alex turned his nose up at the greasy looking short man in front of them. 'No sir. What you are is nothing more than a common charlatan. None of us have ever cast eyes on you! Now, if you'll excuse us we have two giants to defeat.' Stump nodded his head in agreement and they both began to walk past the seemingly deranged, laughing man. Only Hannah looked on with puzzled apprehension but eventually she too followed.

The trio now had their back to Murdoch but he continued to talk regardless. 'Aren't you at least perplexed as to how you were in the air a moment ago and the next thing you knew you awoke on the ground here?'

'Stranger things have happened to us today, believe you me,' said Alex, not even giving him the courtesy of turning to address him.

'Oh really? Like meeting your long lost brother perhaps?' replied Murdoch, ending his question with a click of his fingers. Suddenly the three retreating students stopped dead in their tracks, unable to move their feet as if they had been set fast in concrete.

Murdoch unhurriedly moved around to face them as the shocked youngsters desperately tried to shift their paralysed feet.

'I am surprising even myself at how good I am getting at this hypnosis lark, even if I do say so myself. Those self-help books really are worth every penny. You see, I had thought you might be able to land safely in your bird plane before my powers took effect. That is the only reason I erased your memories of me. I reasoned that if you saw me first you would take evasive action to stop me! Still, I am not sure my powers are going to be strong enough for what I want to do next but I thought I'd give it a shot. After all what have I got to lose? Certainly not a loving family, that's for sure!'

'You plan to hypnotise the giants, don't you?' Hannah snarled at the white-suited man.

Murdoch looked on with mock surprise. 'My my, your brains are even better than your looks my dear! Yes, that is indeed my plan.'

151

'But why? What on earth for?' asked Stump.

'The question is not 'why' but 'why not'! You have all seen how those creatures are virtually indestructible. By some fluke you managed to master the weapon of the ancients but they even survived that. Think what I could do if I could harness their strength and they were under my control. I would be unstoppable!'

'Not if we stop you first!' spat Alex defiantly.

Murdoch threatened to burst out laughing once more but he stifled it as a choke. 'And how exactly do you expect to do that when at the click of a finger I can make you do anything I want? Hypnotism can only take you so far though brother Alex. I don't have real powers like you. When I tied you to the chair I told you I took yours from you but that wasn't true, I was only able to make you believe you were powerless.

'Yesterday I would have said that that would have been enough for me. I wanted to see you again, tell you what I had been through, give you a bit of a scare and let you on your way but then those two giants happened to come along. At first I too was scared of those monsters but then I thought – what would my heroes from the A-team do? Why they would strap those beasts down and use them to overthrow the government! Therefore, that is what I intend to do, once I work out the finer details of course. Ergo, sadly you are all now grains of sand in the oyster of this plan but let's see if we can't make a pearl of a solution out of you all!'

All Alex could do was open and close his mouth like a fish out of water as he leaned forward to gesticulate, unable to compose a coherent response. In truth he, like his two housemates beside him, had run out of things to say and were bereft of ideas.

'Please, stand at ease now my lady and gentlemen alike,' said Murdoch in an attempt at humour. 'Because, if you would please excuse me, I am expecting my two angry giants to be coming this way soon and I would hate to be in their way. Besides, I need to turn my hypnotic disc back on and point it in their direction if I am to put them under my spell.' Off he strode behind them, leaving the helpless friends frozen like flies in a web waiting for the spider to pass their way.

152

Alex craned his neck, trying to see his evil brother as he walked off, hoping that Murdoch was telling the truth this time about his powers never being removed but it was no use, he was directly behind him. Alex even doubted if he could summon the concentration to have the slightest effect. The focus that had been required to summon his car earlier was only possible in the serene surroundings of a small enclosed ice-tower and the experience had tired him greatly. He doubted he could even move a blade of grass under the pressure of two giants appearing over the cliff top at any moment.

Unseen in the gorge below there were indeed stirrings. The now familiar sounds of the two roaring giants were reaching the ears of the housemates, after reverberating off the stony and tree covered valley sides. Murdoch hummed cheerily as he finished placing the giant hypnotic disc behind the stricken students and in a direct line between them and the giants. If the beasts failed to crush their little bodies out of accident or malice, Murdoch had ensured he would hypnotise the great beasts and direct them somnambulantly towards his brother and meddling peers. The housemates needed a miracle and fast as the unkempt thatched hair of one of the giants appeared over the cliff-top.

It was clear from their vociferous bawling that the giants had not been permanently affected by their encounter with the spire weapon. After rousing themselves from concussion, their energetic battle raged on once more. It was the weaker sibling Vincent who climbed up onto the cliff-top first, attempting to gain the higher ground over his brother so he could leap down upon him. The housemates, as yet unnoticed, braced themselves in their helpless position only a few yards away but they were at least temporarily saved from a certain death by Goram who reached up from the valley below to grab the leg of Vincent before he could move away from the cliff edge. Goram dragged his brother back down into the valley and the students allowed themselves to breathe again but their respite was short lived as Vincent again made a break for the higher ground, clambering up the steep valley sides. Goram reached out once more but this time Vincent was able to kick the meaty hand away. He was about to turn and leap back down on top of Goram before he caught sight of the trio of humans but his murderous gaze was very short-lived as he then spied the more captivating image of the spinning disc directly behind where they stood. As Murdoch had predicted, the giant was immediately transfixed and began walking slowly towards the hypnotic device. Goram angrily clambered up the cliff after his brother but his attention was also caught by the mesmeric spinning disk. Both giants were unaware of the small human creatures they were about to crush into the grass and mud only a few mighty steps in front of them.

From the safety of a small hillock nearby, Lance Murdoch looked on, wringing his hands with great mirth and anticipation. He bided the time trying to guess the last thoughts of his brother, wondering if he even hoped for a near impossible salvation, something that had such a low probability of happening it would surely be classed a miracle.

Some statisticians state that once an event has been deemed possible of occurring, it will happen at some point, no matter how small the possibility. Unfortunately for Murdoch, one near improbability was going to happen at a time when he least wanted it to…and that time was now and arrived in the unexpected form of another giant. However this giant did not resemble a human form, but that of a duck!

It was Hannah who first spotted the great bird. It emerged in the sky as a black dot that, as it flew ever nearer, grew into the familiar form they last saw cooped up in the underground cavern. 'The giant duck! He has come to save us!' she said as she clasped her hands together in a rare show of emotion and gratitude for their potential saviour. Embarrassed by the looks from her two companions, she promptly regained her normal composed demeanour, placing her hands in her pockets one more.

The over-sized water fowl approached its landing spot with a graceful glide, its wings rigidly outstretched until the moment before impact when they rotated at increasing speed to control the decent. Ducks never struggle to land on water as they could use lakes and rivers as a relatively long and forgiving landing strip to cushion their weighty feathered derrières. Unfortunately the same could not be said for landings on grass. Therefore the large duck came to rest with a graceless bump and a roll. Whether by design or by happy accident, the final resting place of the giant bird was directly on top of the locally infamous Lance Murdoch and his infuriating rotating disc.

The hypnotic trance now broken, the friends were free to move their legs once more. All three used their stiff limbs immediately and to good effect by running away from the two giants. The beasts themselves momentarily stood still, clearing their heads after their mental invasion. The giant duck did not give the huge figures time to recover though, dismissively swatting each one up and into the air with a whip of its mighty wing. Each one landed next to each other some distance down river, under the old suspension bridge.

'Thank you so much!' said Hannah as she rushed over to greet the huge duck they had met in the caverns earlier that day.

The others walked over more calmly, Alex thinking about what the duck had said in the caverns. 'I thought you were trapped in your cave?' he said with a hint of cynicism, questioning why the huge bird could not have helped much earlier.

'Oh I was,' said the duck. 'Those caverns were built around as me as a prison as my very appearance to the outside world would not be accepted. However the tremors caused by those marauding giants loosened the structure of the cavern enough for me to break out of my underground world just in the last few minutes.'

'Yes, thanks,' murmured Stump, uncomfortable at having to accept help. 'We were just about to do something ourselves of course,' he continued as he flexed his new muscles in an apparent show of strength.

'Indeed. I could see that,' said the duck sarcastically, his booming voice possessing much less timbre out in the open. 'Although, in all seriousness, that is what I came here to do. I came to show you that you will have to help yourselves, I cannot finish the job off for you. I only came here to right a wrong as Murdoch was not foretold in the ancient writings. He was an outside event that would have wrongly tipped the balance of fate against you all.'

'But you have to help us more as I don't know what else we can do to rid us of the giants!' Hannah pleaded. 'I have followed the ancient scriptures to the letter and what good has it done us? Stump and Alex both have new found strengths but it is no match for these huge beasts and the weapon at the church didn't work properly. In short, we are helpless!'

'That is simply not true Hannah,' the duck said, shaking his head. 'You are in control of your own destiny, you always have been, you and everyone who lives in this city. We are not here to help you in your endeavours in life, in your battles. We only made you think that so that you would relax and have the freedom to think for yourselves and work together to overcome these trials and tribulations.'

'That is quite enough,' Stump bleated defiantly. 'I have had it up to here with your ridiculous pomp and unending riddles. I think it is my destiny to wring your bloody neck!' Rolling up his sleeves he stomped over to the giant water dweller but unfortunately for the proud northerner he got nowhere near close enough to grab the duck's jugular as the reach of the duck's mighty wing swung in a great arc, lifting the surprised Stump well off his feet and sending him flying far through the air. He soared over the few strewn and limping ducks that were still nursing their wounds and landed a couple of hundred yards from the group, next to the observatory above the old bridge and near the giants.

'I suggest you heed my words, unlike your hot-headed friend,' said the giant duck solemnly. 'Your lives and probably many more will rely on what you do next.' With that he flew off with a short run and great beating of his wings, filling the turbulent air with that now familiar 'un-cleaned aviary' stench. In the shallow impression left in the ground where the giant duck had squatted, the body of Lance Murdoch lay – alive but crushed in body and in spirit.

Hannah and Alex both stared after the departing bird, their brains trying to come to terms with yet another perplexing happenstance until Hannah took control once more. 'Quick! We must go the bridge!' she said as she started to run off, barely waiting to see if her companion would follow.

'I assume this means you have a plan then? You know what that duck was talking about?'

'No, not at all,' replied a breathless Hannah without breaking her stride. 'But I do know we need to see if Stump is alright and we need to protect him from the giants if, as I fear, they have survived their latest battering.'

No more words were spoken as they quickened their pace for the relatively short run to the north side of the bridge.

Out of breath they reached the suspended crossing together, Alex finally catching up with Hannah. There they recovered before they looked for Stump whilst ensuring they crouched low to avoid the attention of the beasts in case they were alive and awake in the river below.

The final stage was now set for a battle they weren't sure how to fight and even less sure how to win.

26

Hannah was tired as she reached the old suspension bridge that traversed the gorge but at least the run had given her time to think. She knew at last what she had to do and she knew it was the only way. Now recovered from her recent exertions she ran past the ugly concrete toll booth, grabbing the metal railing as she leapt onto the bridge. Full pelt she bounded down the walkway on the western edge, the fragile structure shaking slightly with every footfall. Alex was left at the bridge end, wondering what on earth she was doing now and if he should follow.

Within seconds Hannah reached the half way point of the bridge and began to climb up the netted fencing. She made surprisingly short work of the ascent, despite the top of the fence being angled inwards to deter the occasional suicidal citizen intent on ending their days by plunging to the river below.

With one agile swing, she was now precariously perched on top of the fence, using one of the white vertical support poles to balance herself.

From her lofty position she looked down over the peculiar scene below. Normally at this point in the course of the river the waters would be quiet except for infrequent small vessels passing by but today Hannah stared down onto the thinly thatched pates and swinging arms of two huge brothers hell bent on destroying each other.

Unbeknownst to the heroic trio, they had not been the only ones who had tried to vanquish the giants that day. Too wrapped up in their own adventure, they had not noticed the machinations and might of the military who had also been attempting to slay the fearsome creatures. Although theirs was a belated effort as they had only been made aware of the presence of the giants by members of the media instead of their own intelligence forces who had been 'out to lunch' in every meaning of the phrase.

In a concerted effort to exterminate the beasts, various methods by land, sea and air had been employed but their bodies had proven impervious to guns and missiles alike. All conventional options had been exhausted by man to fight these foes and only one alternative remained that would prove costly to life and limb. It was a choice that, in its last use in anger, effectively ended a global war.

As the drone of a huge lumbering military aircraft could be ominously heard in the distance, Hannah jumped into the air where so many had gone before, the posters for the Samaritans helpline being unread and ignored once more.

At this point Hannah naturally expected gravity to take hold but she found herself unnaturally suspended in mid-air. She was not surprised for long, turning her head slowly towards Alex standing at the end of the bridge. He stood with one arm outstretched in her direction, seemingly preventing her fall with his mind as he outstretched his right arm towards her.

'What on earth are you doing Hannah?' Alex said, clearly perplexed.

'You have to let me go Alex. I have to leave you, just as I did years before. It's the only way. You have to trust me one last time.'

'But you can't. Its suicide!...Wait a minute,' he said. 'What do you mean by 'like I left you before'?'

Hannah now wore a pained, almost guilty expression. She could almost not look Alex in the eyes, eyes that Alex suddenly realised he had not truly looked at in detail before. They were eyes of the most striking icy blue, just like...'Oh my god,' he said, with shock. 'You are the girl from sixth form. The only one that I truly loved and the only one who spurned me!'

'Yes, it is me,' Hannah replied with her head bowed as she floated in the air. 'You wouldn't have understood back then but I could not get involved with anyone, even if I did like you.'

'So you did like me.'

'Yes. I was drawn to you like everyone else had been. I was not immune to your powers but I could not neglect my studies. I could not afford such distractions as I already knew the importance of what fate had laid out before me. I had already discovered the legend of the giants of the gorge and I knew they were due to return now, in a few short years from when you first saw me. I was the only one who could decipher the readings and I could not let anyone or anything jeopardize our salvation.'

'But at least we can be together now?' said Alex, with far more hope than conviction.

'No we can't Alex. Its not our destiny. Lovers depend on meeting at the right place and the right time and I'm afraid we had neither factor in our favour. Trust me Alex. If I am right and the legend is right, I will be just fine when I fall but I'm sorry, we can never be together and you will see exactly why soon enough.' Her voice becalmed Alex even if it did not allay his fears or brighten his dark mood.

'I've worked out the end of the poem Alex,' she continued. 'Don't you remember it ended '*Victory against the giants will be won…*'

'*…Even if one life is given,*' interrupted Alex.

'That's right. I am that life Alex, and there was one last line on that poem that none of us saw, the portion that was incinerated by the napalm-using groundskeeper. However, I somehow knew that I would be able to work out the missing line – not that I was sure how until I had time to think on the run over here to the bridge. I remembered that I had seen the end of the poem elsewhere, on the sign outside the Mason's Arms in fact. The whole poem had been displayed there once but the rest of the lines had been worn away over time until now only the last line remains – *Released to the river, dead and gone.*'

A few minutes earlier, in a secret bunker many miles away beneath central London, important men quietly sat around a table. Discussions had lasted all day and everyone was exhausted. The walls were covered in maps annotated with arrows drawn in every direction and flip-charts had been used to scribble down increasingly desperate notions but now their pages were left where they had been scattered on the table like paintings discarded by a temperamental artist.

The cheap freeze-dried coffee that had barely had the desired caffeine kick earlier in the day was now completely redundant as a pick-me-up. The empty mugs were scattered around the large metal table, leaving rings on the steel surface that the cleaners would 'tut' at later on, never envisaging the gravitas of the decision that was made all the more unpalatable by the bitter coffee the vessels contained.

Silence permeated the air. Everyone had finished talking. Every scenario, strategic angle and flimsy possibility had been examined with associated hopes raised only to be sorely dashed. This had not been the normal way of doing things but this was far from a normal situation. There was no policy or framework written for this most unlikely of events, no guidelines to dutifully follow. They had had to begin from scratch but now in the end the only solution was the one they had feared the most from the start.

Everyone looked at each other and then at the man at the head of the table. He nodded without discernable emotion and slowly picked up the red phone receiver in front of him with reverent care. The phone did not have any buttons to dial. It did not need them as there was only one number this phone would ever have to call. This was its maiden call and everyone in the room prayed inwardly to their various deities that this would be its last.

At the other end of the phone connection, computers (that had only ever been tested and not used in anger) whirred into life, ready to receive the coded instructions. The most important man in the secret bunker said only a few special words into the mouthpiece of the red phone, his voice almost cracking under the strain. The computer verified the short message almost as soon as he replaced the receiver on its hook. In milliseconds the computer had gone through an automated checklist verifying the voice it was 'hearing' and the ciphers used. The instructions were translated into orders and a signal was sent by the computer with electronic efficiency and zero emotion.

A few moments before, at a small airbase in the in the middle of the Wiltshire countryside, a serviceman was on a lonely vigil inside the small missile command centre. (Maps of the area listed the site as 'Disused' but that was actually far from the case. Apart from the government and military 'Top brass' only a few local farmers knew of

161

its active existence and they were kept quiet with a significant reduction on their council tax.)

The serviceman leaned back in his swivel-chair and pulled his cap down over his eyes to get a few minutes shut-eye. Anywhere else in the forces this would not have been possible but he knew this base was used for 'extreme emergencies only' and in peace time he was more likely to see Shegar galloping past the narrow slit window than receive any type of instruction. Today he was going to wish that the most eventful thing to happen would be a missing horse passing by. But alas it was not to be. He woke with a start as an unfamiliar alarm sounded in the small room. It was a loud, unignorable sound accompanied by a specific flashing red light.

He could not believe it. Surely it could not be *that* light. His training meant he knew exactly what to do and he rang the appropriate number, still in disbelief. His face drained as a faceless bureaucrat hastily confirmed it was not a drill. This was for real.

The young man's heart began beating through his rib-cage but with a shaking hand and sweaty fingers he remembered his training and he made the next call. A chain of events was then put into action that resulted in a startled pilot and co-pilot running to their plane that was already being warmed up on the tarmac, a duty officer quickly ticking off each requirement of the pre-flight checklist with a regulation clip-board, his cheap pocket mack protecting his pristine uniform from the light drizzle that floated down from the blanket grey sky.

The plane took off on its short mission with a heavy cargo attached underneath. Inside, the two pilots looked at each other, barely believing what they were about to do on friendly soil.

At the river a new sound gradually began to fill the air. Behind the two housemates the drone of a huge bulbous plane with its deadly payload grew louder and louder as it closed in on its target. Everyone looked up, even the two giants who could not ignore the noise of the flying beast as they stopped exchanging blows for a few moments, even if they had little comprehension of what it was or the threat it posed.

On the bridge, Alex's mental composure began to visibly weaken under the gaze from Hannah. The veneer of his featureless face began to crack and crumble into a pained, miserable expression as his outstretched arm began to tremble.

In the skies above them all, the airmen in the 'state of the art' warplane neared their target. Within seconds they would complete their mission. Never in their lifetimes did they think they would have to detonate such a deadly device and of course it was countless times worse that it was on their own country, their own people. The 'kill zone' had been evacuated as thoroughly as possible but they knew a few stubborn and unbrigaded unfortunates would perish considering the short timescales involved. In fact they could even make out a couple of souls down there on the bridge who had somehow skirted the cordon of armed troops and escaped the enforced exodus. Still, that was not the bigger issue. The airmen knew full well that even if there were no casualties, the ground, air and water would be contaminated for weeks, months and maybe even years to come.

But, when all was said and done, the airmen were professionals and knew they had a job to do for queen and country. They would become known forever as the heroes that stopped the beastly giants but that would be a very hollow accolade. The two pilots looked at each other one last time and nodded as they both flicked up the clear plastic flaps in front of them that protected the flashing red buttons from accidental contact. Neither were men of religion but at that moment they both silently prayed for the words 'ABORT! ABORT! ABORT!' to be screamed through their earphones. They knew that particular moral salvation was diminishing in probability with every lengthy passing second.

Then time ran out. They reached forward in unison, two synchronized thumbs pressing two impatient blinking buttons. Immediately and soundlessly beneath their seats a hatch opened and the bomb dropped, computer guidance ensuring the deadly instrument of warfare would hone in on its pre-programmed quarry. The interior of the plane darkened automatically to protect the aviators from the blinding glow that was about to engulf everything around them as the plane banked hard, speeding away from the impact zone.

At exactly the same time as the bomb fell, Alex finally dropped his arm and relaxed. He let Hannah go but for a moment she stayed there, suspended like a cartoon character before its inevitable plummet.

'Thank you', she whispered before gravity belatedly took hold and she disappeared out of view beneath the bridge. Alex rushed over to the point at the barrier where she had climbed up a few minutes before, his hands clasping the wire mesh as he saw her drop down into the chasm below.

And drop she did, but not in the way any of them expected for as she fell she appeared to slow down, as if her decent was tempered by an invisible cushioning hand. All eyes belonging to man and giant alike were looking now, all from a different vantage point. Guns and missiles hadn't stopped the warring giants but this falling, fluttering damsel who was about come to grief beside them had finally distracted them. Alex watched on from the bridge but his trance was broken by the whistling sound of a bomb following the maiden and gaining speed on her.

In truth Hannah was not slowing. It only appeared that way because she was somehow mysteriously and impossibly growing! First her feet swelled like balloons, the laces of her shoes being pulled out of their eyelets to be freed like eels escaping from portholes on a submerged ship, swimming in undulating waves towards the muddy terrain below. Her trousers strained then split, buttons popping at random intervals like popcorn in a microwave. Her shirt was then torn asunder until only her thick and lengthening russet coloured hair covered her modesty. She was now many times her original size, apparently ceasing her growth spurt just before she hit the ground without harm, her new stature not troubled by the leap from the bridge, the suspended roadway now barely above her head.

The two dumbfounded giants turned around to look at the newcomer who now stood barely a few foot shorter than themselves. Their stares quickly changed from one of confusion to sheer delight. She had returned at last. The maiden they had rescued and then fought over almost to the death all that time ago. Avona!

164

No creature, man or beast alike had time to celebrate the new arrival or be bewildered by the latest twist in events as the bomb neared its target. Despite the danger Alex was determined not to let his new re-found and unrequited love die from the impending bomb blast, even if she had now been transformed to a giant. Alex raised his arms toward the huge silvery weapon that gleamed and twinkled, reflecting rays of sunlight as it fell. He was unsure at first if his mental skills could affect the bomb but as he concentrated with all his will, limbs shaking with the tension and pressure, he realised he was having an effect on the weapon! The torpedo-shaped missile first slowed as if the air was thickening before it, then, in mid-air directly in front of him, it ground to a halt. Success was, however, short lived as ominously its point began to pivot, turning away from the giants below that now numbered three, following an arc until Alex could see straight down the length of the red needle at the front end of the device, its bulbous shape following behind it. The bomb shimmered with an aura as its own engine eschewed hot gases, the propulsive force negated exactly by Alex's will power. He was exhausted but the job was less than half done. Somehow he had to turn the hovering machine far away and up in to the skies so it harmlessly exploded into the stratosphere when its internal timer ran to zero.

In the air far above, the pilots looked at each other in confusion once more. They had braced themselves against the shockwaves and blinding light of an explosion that never came. Their instruments now flashed 'MALFUNCTION' in synchrony with an unnecessary buzzing. Most bizarrely, their screens were showing the bomb had not reached the target but was suspended several yards from the ground. The crew continued to return to base, suspecting a computer error. After all, they were safe in the knowledge that if the device had hit the ground and not detonated then the back-up timer would ignite the weapon and finish off those fearsome creatures.

At the bridge, Alex was starting to win his battle. He even afforded himself a smile and a small chuckle as he saw the bomb reluctantly but surely reversing before gaining speed in the right direction, up and past the tree-line and into the azure sky.

Not too far away, a weary, bruised but safe Jack Stump looked on from the safety of the observatory on the raised hill above the valley.

He had awoken on the grass outside, confused but conscious after a concussion caused by the cruel swatting at the hands (or more exactly wings) of the giant duck and his subsequent landing on the forgiving grass where he still laid. Initially he was disorientated and could not see either his housemates or the giants but he knew the observatory in front of him could help him find them as it provided panoramic views of the surrounding area. He rushed into the small stone structure, galloping upstairs to use the camera obscurer in a bid to find friend and foe.

Stump tilted the giant dish pivoted at chest height in front of him to focus in on the events he now discovered unfolding just a few hundred yards away. Using his strength he was able to sway the heavy bowl one way and another, like prospecting for gold from an oversized pan, the reflected image of the outside world gracefully gliding in front of his eyes. Trees, river and bridge flashed past unerringly with a slight distortion that caused some nausea. Finally he could make out the smaller images of people, hazily depicted as if a cheese-cloth was placed over the lens. Stump could do nothing about the grainy picture but the image was clear enough to make out the small figure of Alex, arm pointing towards a glistening metallic shape hovering just in front of him. Despite the poor resolution he could just see the pointed shape as it started to ascend, occasionally glistening as it reflected the sun on its gently rising trajectory. Stump slumped a little as he relaxed with the happy sight, unaware how tight his muscles had become with the tension. But then, suddenly everything reversed. The small gleaming object stopped gaining height and silently began to fall faster and faster towards the ground. He could see Alex dropping his arms and running, his mind telling his body to run despite the overwhelming instinct that any action would be in vain. Stump gripped the side of the metal dish tightly, frozen with fear and helplessness. At least he knew none of his housemates would feel any pain and indeed neither would he. The obliterating shock wave from the nuclear bomb would pass his way in a fraction of a second. His last truncated thought was that of his father, staring at him with hammer and chisel in hand next to the half built house that would be their home. His father soon averted his gaze, looking down at his feet as he shook his head in shame. In his vision Stump knew he had failed his father and everyone else. Stump almost welcomed the bright white light that engulfed the grainy picture in front of him, milliseconds later enveloping him and the observatory, reducing everything in its path to super-heated vapour.

Down by the suspension bridge the scene was one of complete annihilation. Alex barely made it a few steps into his run before being slammed in the back by the enormous force of the explosion in the river below, his remnants being catapulted in all directions. Bizarrely, only his Gap pullover survived, the smoking garment coming to rest intact next a bemused leek farmer many miles away on a Welsh hillside.

The bridge itself had buckled, snapped in half and melted, all within a couple of seconds. At the base of the explosion the muddy river was boiled dry in an instant, a huge crater of molten rock being formed out of the riverbed.

The angry blast of the explosion continued to sweep forward in all directions, wiping out everything in its path. The trees on either side of the gorge were knocked over like matchsticks with the force and were instantly turned to charcoal. Animals stood no chance either, trapped with nowhere to go as their flesh fried and charred before their bones disintegrated. Even the very air was swallowed by the sphere of deadly gases that grew exponentially as a deadly, boiling tidal wave extended west and east along the river, steam replacing water at a frightening rate.

Within seconds the explosion had reached the mighty river Severn in the west and the centre of Bristol in the east where fiery gale-force winds cooked any human unlucky or foolish enough not to have joined the evacuation. For minutes that whole corner of the world held its breath as a toxic grey dust rained down in clumps like a dirty snowfall. The only sounds came from the odd fire that lazily licked at the few remaining flammable items that protruded from the wasteland and toppling buildings that inevitably lost their integrity in the face of intense heat and furious winds.

Then, after more time had passed, some people did appear. They weld their way towards the centre of the devastation in armoured vehicles and suits to guard them against the arid, burning landscape. Reaching their destination the figures reluctantly left the safety of their protected capsules in the vain search for survivors. They held out instruments before them but their reactions to the readings they took was indiscernible through their tough, opaque visors.

Stump awoke with a start from his nightmare, gasping for air, fully believing he was in the midst of the nuclear inferno. (The closest he had actually come to such a holocaust was to nearly set his eyebrows on fire as his smouldering pipe had rested next to his hairy, unkempt head.)

He slapped his hands on the image in front of him that was projected onto the dish, expecting to see devastation in front of him. But no, all he saw was Alex standing with arm outstretched pointing towards the motionless bomb, just as he had seen before.

At first Stump thought he had somehow gone back in time but after a moment he came to his senses. His apocalyptic visions had all been another dream, another premonition, but this time surely he had a chance to change the future if he could use his strength to help Alex deflect the bomb?

The old wooden door to the observatory almost flew off its hinges as Stump's sturdy arm flung it aside. He careered from the circular stone building, almost slipping on the wet grass outside as he flew towards the cliff edge. In one deft swinging movement he grabbed hold of the rusting metal railing and flung himself underneath, slithering down the locally famous diagonal rock made smooth by generations of children using it as a natural slide. Landing on his feet at its base he bounded past the small toll-booth at the start of the bridge, arms pumping in time with his powerful legs, eager to help out his friends whilst they all still had time. Presently he reached the others and slowed his pace to stare in wonder at the scene before him, the bomb floating in the air as Alex struggled to stop its progression. Even from some yards away the strain was etched on the young man's face as the explosive device remained stubbornly in position. Stump watched on with hope, not wanting to charge forward until he felt it was absolutely necessary in case he risked breaking the concentration of his housemate.

The situation was clearly a stalemate, two warring factions both waiting for the other to give in. Man against machine. But wait! Suddenly, almost imperceptibly, the bomb began to move upwards into the sky! Stump relaxed as he could see his friend from the south also slacken his mental grip. They both started to laugh as the bomb almost disappeared out of view but their joy was short lived. The strain reappeared on Alex's face, the frosting in his hair shaking with tension like a bush covered in snow quivering in the wind. Alex stepped back as if being flattened underneath an invisible weight before he finally stumbled and fell, knocking himself unconscious on the tarmac surface of the bridge. Stump rushed forward to help his stricken pal but then stopped dead when he saw the bomb that was once again propelling itself downwards towards its target, just as in his premonition.

The Yorkshire lad looked around him for anything he could use to stop the explosive device. Suddenly he had a brainwave. He knew what he could do. At great speed the burly boy rushed over to a sturdy looking (and crucially straight) young willow tree some four and a quarter inches wide that lazily grew out of the steep hillside. Using his recently increased strength he stooped low, encircled the trunk with his thick forearms and wrenched it clear from the ground in one clean jerk, roots and all.

As Stump raced back to the epicentre of the unfolding events, nimbly carrying the plucked tree over his shoulder, he reflected for the first time that his father was wrong about many things. He just hoped that this revelation had not been too late.

He knew his dad was not an evil man, he had just become bitter and twisted after what he thought was the betrayal of Stump's mother. It was that that had forced him to bring his son up in his image, imposing his own views and ways on him, hoping that his progeny could change the world into his biased way of thinking. Ironically it had been a woman, Hannah, who had shown him the error of his ways and how females could actually be the equal of men and that not all modern vices were necessarily a bad thing. At least his father had taught him one useful, vital and noble skill that might just save them all.

Stump now stood in position at the edge of the bridge with the mighty trunk of the willow tree in his hand. He faced the gently descending bomb side on and thoughtfully tapped the base of the tree against the soft ground a couple of times.

The weighty northerner began to dream again but this was a different type of reverie. He bent over, half-crouched, poised like a coiled python waiting for the right moment to strike its pray. The bomb was now arcing directly towards him but Stump saw a very different scene. In his eyes he was a young boy again standing on the lush green hills of the moors, one of the rare happy times in his childhood. In the distance he could see the colourful pattern of his mother's dress calling him in for dinner from the doorway of their simple home. 'Just one more over!' he pleaded, not even looking in her direction, too focused to take his eyes from the bowler some 22 yards away. The bowler duly steamed up to the wicket, his tongue firmly held between his teeth with concentration as his arms wheeled around in the familiar windmill fashion. A looping medium-paced delivery emerged out of the darkening sky and the young Stump swung with his bat at the perfect moment. The pleasing cracking sound of willow hitting leather rang out as the ball disappeared just over his father's head causing him to duck. The boy was then worried that his father may be angry at the shot that nearly connected soundly with his head. The younger Stump winced and prepared to be chided but the older man merely laughed with pleasant surprise and even clapped the effort of his offspring. Such a rare showing of fatherly love made so much of a difference to the young scamp that he beamed inside and out for hours until he finally fell asleep that night.

The view changed once again in front of Stump's eyes. The sky remained the same but the grass in front of him gave way to the chasm of the gorge and the old stone wall of his childhood home was now the base of the old bridge. Arcing away from him was the bomb and by his side was the busted remains of the willow tree, split in two by the impact after it had made contact with the missile.

Down in the valley beneath the bridge, the three giants stood. Now that the threat of the bomb had been removed they all looked at each other warily, fully aware what had happened last time they were all together.

Avona and Goram desperately wanted to embrace but Goram feared the reaction of his brother. He even felt a twinge in his back and instinctively rubbed the area where his brother's axe had wedged in that fateful moment that was recreated each millennia. The two reunited lovers tensed as they waited for Vincent's reaction but before they could gauge his emotions they were all distracted once more by a descending whistling sound above their heads. The bomb that Stump had batted away had not reached the proverbial boundary rope and now fatefully careered back towards the giants. Above them the bedraggled humans could only look on, exhausted and forlorn, their own super-human efforts clearly being in vain.

Instinctively Goram rushed towards to bomb to protect the others, not truly understanding what the projectile was but sensing the danger it presented. As he ran he almost slipped in the soft mud but found his footing once more only to find Vincent blocking his path. Goram sprang to the right to go around his sibling, looking up to make sure he was still on course to meet the deadly device dropping from the sky but as he did so Vincent heftily pushed his running sibling out of the way. Goram was sent flying, landing and sliding some yards in the brown mud. Avona shrieked and fell to her knees, fearing that Vincent had once again dashed their slim hopes of survival. She was not looking forward to another thousand years of separation and incarceration from her beloved.

Vincent took one last loving look at Avona, the woman he wanted so much but again would not have. He turned on his heels and stealthily ran after the bomb, lunging forward, catching the contraption deftly in his fingertips and running on once more, this time away from his brother, away from Avona and everyone else. In a few seconds he was a mere blip against the western skyline as he headed towards the great river Severn and beyond that, the sea.

Another couple of minutes passed before a shimmering flash of light could be seen on the western horizon. At first it looked like a second yellow sun, an untimely sunrise at the opposite point of the compass. The new sun grew and grew and then appeared to implode in on itself, shrouded by a hazy veil of vapour that funnelled up from an unseen point on the surface of the sea. The huge ethereal mushroom then dissolved as a deep rumble began to build. What started as a whisper soon matured until the very earth appeared to groan with almighty force. Only when the incredible sound had died down did hope start to blossom amongst those standing around the bridge and further afield. In time this hope was replaced by relief that everyone was still alive but it was much longer before the people of the once great city would return to rebuild and re-evaluate their lives.

The story of Goram, Vincent and Avona had ended but the tale and its lessons would be retold in pubs over a couple of ales, from parent to child at the bedside, by reverends from the pulpit and by politicians to its constituents.

Epilogue

The city of Bristol did manage to repair itself after what later became known as 'The Battle of the Giants.' The buildings and streets were rebuilt, the homeless housed and in almost every way, the lives of the general populous continued on in the same ways as they ever had. But some things would never be the same. The attitudes of the people living in the city were changed forever and a few more than most.

All the main protagonists learned major lessons during the unfolding of their tale and all realised it should not have taken such a traumatic event to show them the error of their ways and means.

The housemates in the tale all went on to pass their degrees with varying levels of success but parted ways shortly after. They stayed in touch with the odd phone call and naff Christmas card but rarely more. They all felt a rendezvous would open up the wounds that were still all too fresh.

Alex never fully retained his powers of influence after his super-human effort to try to deflect the bomb. He was either too reluctant or simply unable to repeat those feats. However, he did enjoy the limelight his new fame briefly afforded him, appearing on a couple of television chat-shows where he levitated a few Z-list celebrities (amongst other trivialities) but the media soon grew bored of him and him of it.

He learned that other skills were just as effective, such as using his confidence to set himself up as an entrepreneur, literally selling coals to Newcastle, ice to Eskimos and sand to Timbuktu. He even found love, not only in the voluptuous shapes of the frankly daring new range of Bristol blue glass but also in that of a woman who he eventually settled down with after begrudgingly learning how to share his personal space and time.

Years later he even finally understood why Hannah was so sure she had to sacrifice herself. One day he noticed that the Mason's Arms was finally being renovated and the curious sign repainted. He happened to be walking past when a local artist was re-painting the words on the faded scroll, revealing the full poem. He saw that Hannah had been telling the truth and that her fate really was spelt out for her. The bold capital letters of each line on the scripted poem suddenly made the message jump out at him. A new missive could be constructed from the first letter of each line of the poem – '*Hannah falls into Avon River.*'

Following the ancient instructions to the letter, she had swapped her mortal life for one of eternity in her former existence as Avona. Maybe she realised that if the legend was not true and she stayed as Hannah, Alex would surely have rescued her with his powers before she plunged to her death in the muddy river. No one will ever know, he mused as he decided to walk inside the pub for old time's sake and enjoy a pint of ale, avoiding eye-contact with other patrons and the rat-flavoured cider obviously.

Stump spent time getting to know his mother, a happy time for both parties. He also was awarded 'National Tea-drinker' of the year on no less than four consecutive occasions and settled down in a small semi-detached somewhere in 'The North'. He made a fair living making appearances on television quiz shows and decorated his new house with comfortable meagre furniture. (The colour palette used for the interior of his abode consisted entirely of slightly different shades of beige and that was the way he liked it. It seemed the influence of some of his father's dour ways were, in the end, too hard to shift.) The only concession to colour was an ornate teapot in the shape of an elephant, the trunk of the animal obviously being the spout. It was a gift from his mother.

Murdoch found solace after his showdown with his brother Alex. However, he could never quite live with the modern world even after finding his peace so he purchased a 'retro' shop in a bohemian part of Bristol, funded by a kind donation from Alex. For a while this made Murdoch happy, spending hours ensconced in his shop, surrounded by telephones shaped liked lobsters, faded leather jackets, stone-washed jeans and Atari 64 games consoles. But after a year he realised he still did not feel at home and he needed to move to somewhere that was still stuck in the 1980's just like him, so he emigrated to New Zealand.

The once goodly Reverend Gooding never found his calling again. He had lost his faith well before the events of that autumn afternoon in his church. Instead he took the opposite path…in more ways than one. He moved to London where he found a job teaching about evolution to schoolchildren at the Natural History Museum and had a revelation of another type, becoming an active member of the gay scene in nearby Soho, where he could be often seen on a Friday night, arm in arm with his new squeeze Phil.

Levi, the less than handsome barman at the Mason's Arms, profited handsomely from the episode. He surprised everyone by using his very well hidden entrepreneurial skills to make a tourist attraction of the grotto that now adjoined the main bar. He also found the conditions were perfect for stilling his lethal moonshine that he served to locals 'in the know' who would ask for the odd snifter with a sideways nod and a tap of their reddening noses.

Dusty Green was just grateful for not having any more mysterious holes undermining his cricket pitch. He didn't have to use napalm again to rid the earth of pests, mole-like or otherwise, but he never did quite regain the bowling green like surface he had honed over decades of care. He was not forlorn though as the now uneven pitch helped their spin bowlers to a hat-full of wickets the following summer, much to the chagrin of the visiting batsmen who would never know that a giant duck rested several yards underneath the wicket.

Last, but in so many ways not least, the giants of the gorge lay in their resting place once again. Their revenge resolved and their story over they were re-absorbed by the rocks that saw their rebirth. They will surely rise again in another millennia to re-enact their tale but with hope they will have learnt from this episode that only one of them can place the hand of fair Avona in their own. But at least for now they can rest in peace and so can the residents of Bristol, including the ducks who will bide their time in the thousands of ponds and rivers of the city, hoping that one day the bread they are thrown is not quite so stale. Is a little fresh ciabatta really too much to ask for?